Dear Reader,

It is so interesting to look back at *The Cowboy and the Lady,* first published in 1982. It was written, however, in 1981, a momentous year in my life. Our son, Blayne, was just a year old. I was still working as a full-time newspaper reporter, on call twenty-four hours a day and writing books at night after I got off work. My husband, James, was working at a clothing manufacturing company. We drove a ten-year-old car, had very little money, lived in a rented house and watched the baby as much as we watched television for entertainment.

Twenty-seven years later Blayne is married and his wife, Christina, is expecting *their* first child. We are living in a home we own, not rent, and the car in the driveway is a very fast new Jaguar. I still work full-time, and have no plans to retire, ever. Like Harlequin Books, I seem to have the gift of endurance.

Harlequin is now sixty years old. I myself am also into my sixth decade. I am still filled with wonder when I think about the wonderful job I have—one I would gladly do for nothing.

I owe this to a lot of people: my husband and son, who put up with a lot of cold dinners; and my best friend, Ann, without whom I would never have sent off that first manuscript. To my extraordinary editor, Tara Gavin, and my agent Maureen Walters. And last but never least, my loyal readers who are very much a part of my life. They are my family. So is Harlequin and its amazing staff. All of us together, writers and others, make up this wonderful company, which has never lost its special touch as the oasis of pure romance in the world.

Congratulations, Harlequin, on your Diamond Anniversary. I hope that you, and I, will continue to warm the hearts of women around the world with love stories that never go out of style. And thank you from the bottom of my heart for giving me a job in the first place.

With all best wishes to our readers everywhere,

Diana Palmer

Praise for *New York Times* bestselling author Diana Palmer

"Nobody does it better."
—*New York Times* bestselling author Linda Howard

"Palmer's talent for character development and ability to fuse heartwarming romance with nail-biting suspense shine in *Outsider.*"
—*Booklist*

"Diana Palmer is a mesmerizing storyteller who captures the essence of what a romance should be."
—*Affaire de Coeur*

"The dialogue is charming, the characters likable and the sex sizzling."
—*Publishers Weekly* on *Once in Paris*

"No one beats this author for sensual anticipation."
—*Rave Reviews*

"A love story that is pure and enjoyable."
—*Romantic Times BOOKreviews* on *Lord of the Desert*

"Palmer knows how to make the sparks fly.... Heartwarming."
—*Publishers Weekly* on *Renegade*

THE HARLEQUIN FAMOUS FIRSTS COLLECTION™

NEW YORK TIMES BESTSELLING AUTHOR

DIANA PALMER

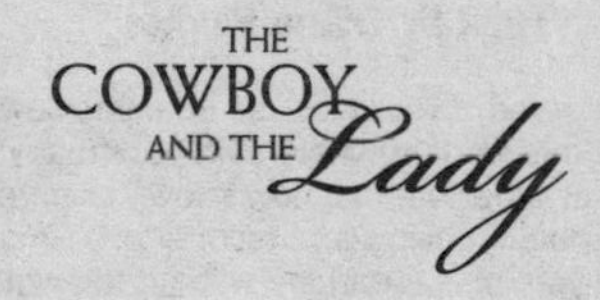

TORONTO • NEW YORK • LONDON
AMSTERDAM • PARIS • SYDNEY • HAMBURG
STOCKHOLM • ATHENS • TOKYO • MILAN • MADRID
PRAGUE • WARSAW • BUDAPEST • AUCKLAND

To Frances Thompson and family

Recycling programs for this product may not exist in your area.

ISBN-13: 978-0-373-20008-5

THE COWBOY AND THE LADY

This edition published by arrangement with Harlequin Books S.A.

www.eHarlequin.com

Printed in U.S.A.

Chapter One

They were at a standstill, the tall man and the willowy young blonde, poised like boxers waiting for an opening.

"Never!" she repeated, her brown eyes throwing off sparks. "I know we need the business, and I'd do anything for you—within reason. But this isn't reasonable, and you know it, Terry Black!"

He drew a weary breath and turned to the window overlooking San Antonio's frantic late-morning traffic, his hands rammed into his pockets, his thin shoulders slumping dejectedly.

"I'll be ruined," he said softly.

She glared at his back. "Sell one of your Cadillacs," she suggested.

He threw her an irritated glance. "Amanda…!"

"I was Mandy when I came in this morning," she reminded him, tossing back her long, silver-blond hair with a smile. "Come on, Terry, it isn't all that bad."

"No," he agreed finally, "I guess it isn't." He leaned back against the wall beside the huge picture window and let his eyes drift over her soft, young curves, lingering where her beige shirtwaist dress made a straight line across the high, small curve of her breasts. "He can't really dislike you," he added absently. "No man with blood in his veins could."

"Jason Whitehall doesn't have any blood in his veins," she said. "He has ice water and a dash of aged whiskey."

"Jason didn't offer me the account. His brother Duncan did."

"Jace owns the lion's share of the corporation, though, Terry," she argued. "And he's never used an advertising agency, not ever."

"If the Whitehalls want to sell lots in that inland development project they're working on in Florida, they'll have to use one. And why not us?" he added with a boyish grin. "After all, we're the best."

She threw up her slender hands. "So you keep telling me."

"We need the account," he persisted. His thin, boyish face grew thoughtful. "Do you realize just how big the Whitehall empire is?" he asked, as if she'd never heard of it. "The Texas ranch alone covers twenty-five thousand acres!"

"I know." She sighed, and her soft brown eyes were sad with memory. "You forget, my father's ranch adjoined the Whitehalls' before—" She broke off. "Anyway, it's not as if you couldn't go by yourself."

He looked briefly uncomfortable. "Uh, I'm afraid I can't do that."

She blinked at him across the luxurious carpeted room

with its modern chrome-trimmed furniture. "I beg your pardon?"

"It's no deal unless you come along."

"Why?"

"Because we're partners," he said stubbornly, his lower lip thrusting forward. "And mostly because Duncan Whitehall won't discuss it without you. He's considering our agency because of his friendship with you. How about that? *He* came looking for *us*."

That was strange. She and Duncan had been friends for many years, but knowing how his brother felt, it was odd that he'd insist on her presence for business.

"But Jace hates me," she murmured, wide-eyed. "I don't want to go, Terry."

"Why does he hate you, for heaven's sake?" he asked, exasperated.

"Most recently," she admitted, "because I ran over his quarter-million-dollar bull."

"Come again?"

"Well, I didn't actually do it. Mother did, but she was so afraid of Jace that I took the blame. It didn't endear me to him, either—he was a grand champion."

"Jace?"

"The bull!" She folded her arms across her chest. "Mother can't accept the fact that the old days, when we had money, are gone. I do. I can stand alone. But she can't. If she wasn't able to visit Marguerite at Casa Verde for several weeks a year, and pretend nothing has changed, I'm not sure she could manage." She shrugged. "Jace hated me anyway. It just gave him a better reason to let him think I crippled the animal."

"When did all this happen?" he asked curiously. "You

never mentioned it after your trip…of course, you looked like death warmed over for a couple of weeks, and I was head over heels with that French model…."

She smiled. "Exactly."

He sighed. "Well, it doesn't change things, anyway. If you don't go with me, we forfeit the account."

"We may forfeit it anyway, if Jace has his way," she reminded him. "It's only been six months. I promise you he hasn't gotten over it."

His pale eyes narrowed. "Amanda, are you really afraid of him?"

She smiled wanly. "I didn't realize it showed."

"That's a first," he observed, amused. "You aren't the shrinking violet type, and I've seen that sweet temper of yours a time or two in the past year." His lips pursed. "Why are you afraid of him?"

She turned away. "Now, there, my friend, is a question. But I'm afraid I don't have an answer."

"Does he hit?"

"Not women," she said. "I've seen him deck a man, though." She winced at the memory.

"Over a woman?" he fished, grinning.

She averted her eyes. "Over me, actually. One of the Whitehalls' hands got a little too friendly with me to suit Jace, and he gave him a black eye before he fired him. Duncan was there, too, but he hadn't got his mouth open before Jace jumped in. Trying to run my life, as usual," she added unfairly.

"I thought Jace was an old man."

"He is," she said venomously. "Thirty-three and climbing fast."

He laughed at her. "Ten whole years older than you."

She bristled. "I can see what fun this trip is going to be."

"Surely he's forgotten the bull," he said comfortingly.

"Do you think so?" Her eyes clouded. "I had to watch Jace shoot him after the accident. And I'll never forget how he looked or what he said to me." She sighed. "Mother and I ran for our lives, and I drove all the way home in a borrowed car." The skirt of her dress swirled gracefully around her long, slender legs as she turned away. "It was a lot of fun, with a sprained wrist, too, I'll tell you that."

"Don't you believe in burying the hatchet?"

"Sure. So does Jace—about two inches deep at the peak of my forehead…."

"How about if you go home and pack?" he suggested with a grin.

"Home." She laughed softly. "Only you could call that one-bedroom efficiency apartment a home. Mother hates it so. I suppose that's why she spends her life visiting old friends." Visiting. There was another word for it: sponging, and Jace never tired of using it. If he'd had any idea that Beatrice Carson, not her daughter, had steered that car broadside into Duke's Ransom, he'd have thrown her out for good, despite all his mother's fiery protests.

"She isn't at the Whitehall place now?" Terry asked uneasily, visions of disaster clouding his pale eyes.

Amanda shook her head. "It's spring. That means the Bahamas." Beatrice had a schedule of sorts about where she visited and when. Right now she was with Lacey Bannon and her brother Reese. But Marguerite Whitehall's turn was coming up soon, and Amanda was already afraid for her. If Beatrice let anything slip about that stupid bull while she was on the ranch…

"Maybe Duncan will protect me," she murmured wistfully. "Since it was his idea to drag me out to Casa Verde. And I thought he was my friend," she groaned.

Terry toyed with a stack of photographs on his neat desk. "You're not really sore at me, are you?"

She shrugged. "I don't know yet. But if Jace turns thumbs down on the account, don't blame me. Duncan should have let you handle it. I'll only jinx you."

"No, you won't," he promised. "You won't regret it."

She glanced at him over her shoulder with a wry smile. "That's exactly what Mother said when she coaxed me into going to Casa Verde six months ago. I hope your predictions are more accurate than hers were."

Late that night she sat curled up in her comfortable old armchair long after the prime time shows had gone off, watching a news program that she didn't really see. Her eyes were on a photograph in an album, a color snapshot of two men: one tall, one short; one solemn, one smiling. Jace and Duncan, on the steps of the big Victorian mansion at Casa Verde with its green trim and huge white columns and sprawling wide front porch scattered with heavy rocking chairs and a swing. Duncan was smiling, as usual. Jace was openly glaring at the camera, his dark, hard face drawn into a brooding scowl, his eyes glittering like new silver under light. Amanda shivered involuntarily at that glare. She'd been holding the camera, and the glare had been for her.

If only there were some way out of this trip, she thought wildly. If only she could lock the door and put her head under the pillow and make it all go away. If only her father were still alive to control Beatrice. Bea was like a child, backing away from reality like a butterfly from an outstretched hand. She hadn't even protested when Amanda took the blame for hitting the bull and brought Jace's wrath onto her head. She sat right there and let her daughter take the responsibility for it, just as she'd let her take the responsibility for dozens of similar incidents.

And Jace had been given reason to hate her mother long before that accident. But Amanda was too tired to think about that, too. It seemed that she spent her life protecting Bea. If only some kind, demented man would come along and marry her vivacious little headache and take it away to Alaska, or Tahiti, or lower Siberia....

She took one last look at the Whitehall brothers before she closed the album. Now why had Duncan insisted that she come with Terry? They were partners in the ad agency, but Terry was the senior partner and he had the lion's share of experience. She frowned. Of course, Marguerite liked her, and she might have put a bug in Duncan's ear. She smiled. That must be the explanation.

She leaned back in the chair and closed her eyes while the newscaster blared away about a recent murder in the city. His voice began to fade in and out, and before she realized it, she was fast asleep.

Chapter Two

Amanda watched the Victoria airport loom up on the horizon as the pilot of the air taxi banked for his final approach. This part of Texas was no stranger to her. It had been her home before she settled in San Antonio, where she'd gone to college. She'd spent her childhood here, among cattlemen and businessmen and bluebells and an historical legacy that could still make her heart race.

She clenched her hands in her lap. She loved this state, from its western desert fringes to the lush portion of eastern Texas they were now flying over. From Victoria, it was only a short drive to the Whitehall ranch, Casa Verde, and the small community called Whitehall Junction that had sprung up at the edge of the massive property Jace Whitehall had accumulated.

"So this is your hometown?" Terry asked as the small plane touched gently down on the runway with a brief skidding sound before the wheels settled.

"Yes, Victoria," she laughed, feeling her childhood again as she remembered other trips, other landings. "The friendliest little city you've ever seen. I've always loved it here. My father's people settled in this area when it was still dangerous to go riding without a gun. One of Jace's ancestors was a Comanche," she added absently. "It was his uncle who owned Casa Verde. Jace's father, Jude Whitehall, inherited it when the boys were very young."

"You became good friends, I gather?" he asked.

She flushed. "On the contrary. My mother didn't even want me to associate with them. They were only middle class at that time," she added bitterly, "and she never let them forget it. It's a miracle that Marguerite ever forgave her. Jace didn't."

"I begin to see the tip of the iceberg," he chuckled.

They climbed down out of the plane and Amanda drank in the clean air and sun and endless horizon beyond the Victoria skyline.

"No small town, this," Terry said, following her gaze.

"The population is sixty thousand or so," she told him. "One of my grandfathers is buried in Memorial Square. That's the oldest cemetery here, and a lot of pioneer families are buried there. There's a zoo, and a museum, and even a symphony orchestra. Not to mention some of the most delightful concerts—the Bach Festival Concerts are held in June. And there are some old mission ruins—"

"I only made a comment," he interrupted, laughing. "I didn't ask for a community profile."

She smiled at him. "Don't you want to know that it's located on the Guadalupe River?"

"Thank you." He shaded his eyes against the sun. "Who's going to meet us?"

She didn't want to think about that. "Whoever's got time," she said and hoped that ruled out Jace. "Ordinarily, Duncan or Jace would probably have flown to San Antonio after us. They've got two planes, and they're both pilots. They have their own airstrip and hangars, but it's spring," she said, as if that explained everything.

He blinked. "Come again?"

"Roundup," she said. "When they cull and brand and separate cattle. The ranch manager bears the brunt of the responsibility for it, but Jace doesn't turn over all the authority to anyone. He likes to keep his eye on the operation. And that means Duncan has to double up on the real estate interests and the other companies while Jace is occupied here."

"And time is short," Terry said, pressing his lips together. "I didn't think about that, or I'd have been willing to wait until next month. The thing is," he sighed, "we really need this account. Business hasn't been all that good during the winter, the economy's in such a slump."

She nodded, but she wasn't really hearing him. Her eyes were glued to the road leading to the airport, on a silver Mercedes speeding toward them. Jace drove a silver Mercedes.

"You look faintly terrified," Terry remarked. "Recognize that car, do you?"

She nodded, feeling her heartbeat triple as the car came closer and pulled up in front of the terminal. The door swung open and she breathed a sigh of abject relief.

Marguerite Whitehall came toward them in a dressy pink pantsuit and sandals, her white hair faultlessly arranged, her thin face beaming with a smile.

"It's lovely to see you again, dear," she told Amanda as

she hugged her, wrapping her in the delicious scent of Nina Ricci and pressed powder.

"It's good to be here," she lied, meeting the older woman's dark eyes. "This is Terrance Black, my partner at the advertising agency in San Antonio," she introduced him.

"You're very welcome, Terrance," Marguerite said courteously. "Duncan explained the offer you've made. I do hope Jace will go along with it. It's just good business sense, but my eldest has some peculiar ideas about… things," she said with an apologetic smile at Amanda.

"I'm anxious to talk with Duncan about the account," Terry said with a smile.

"He isn't here right now, I'm sorry to say," came the polite reply. "He had to fly to San Francisco this afternoon on some urgent business. But Jace is home."

Amanda felt something give way inside her, and she fought back the urge to leap back aboard the plane and go home. Instead, she followed the two of them to the car and allowed herself to be placed in the front seat with Marguerite while Terry loaded their bags and got in the back seat.

"The weather's nice," Terry commented as Marguerite headed the sleek little car toward the city.

"But dry this year." Marguerite sighed. She didn't go into the various ways droughts played havoc with a ranch. Amanda already knew, and it would have taken the better part of an hour to explain it to someone who wasn't familiar with cattle.

"I'm looking forward to seeing the ranch," Terry volunteered.

Marguerite smiled over her shoulder at him. "We're rather proud of it. I'm sorry you had to take a commercial flight. Jace could have come after you, but Tess was with him, and I didn't think you'd care for her company," she added with a wry glance at Amanda.

"Tess?" Terry probed.

"Tess Anderson," Marguerite replied. "Her father and Jace are partners, with Duncan of course, in that real estate venture in Florida."

"Will we have to consult him about the account as well?" Terry asked.

"I shouldn't think so," the older woman replied conversationally. "He always goes along with whatever Jace says."

"How is Tess?" Amanda asked quietly.

"Just the same as always, Amanda," came the haunted reply. "With one hand reaching out toward Jace eternally."

Amanda remembered that. Tess had always been a step away from him, since they were in their teens. Jace had offered to take Amanda to a dance once—a mysterious offer that Amanda had refused in silent terror. Tess had got wind of it, and given Amanda the very devil, as if it had been her fault that Jace asked her.

"Tess and Amanda were at school together," Marguerite told Terry. "In Switzerland, you know."

It seemed like a hundred years ago. Amanda's family had lost everything when Bob Carson was caught with his financial fingers in a crooked land deal. The shock of discovery had caused a fatal heart attack, and he'd died leaving his stunned wife and daughter to deal with the monumental disgrace and debt. By the time the creditors were satisfied there was nothing left, Jace had offered to help. Amanda still blushed when she remembered exactly how he'd presented the cold-blooded proposition to her.

She'd never told anyone about it. But the memory was still with her, and she'd always believed her refusal had fanned Jace's contempt.

After the ranch went on the auction block, Amanda had carried her journalism degree to Terry Black's office, and the association rapidly became a partnership. The job kept the wolf from the door, when Bea wasn't on a marathon spending spree and so long as she imposed on her wealthy friends with long visits. The sacrificing was all on Amanda's part, not on her mother's. Bea liked pretty clothes and shoes, and she bought them impulsively, always apologizing for her lapses and bursting into tears if Amanda was stern with her. Every day of her life Amanda thanked God for time payments. And every other day, she wondered if Bea was ever going to grow up.

"I said, how's Bea?" Marguerite prompted gently, breaking into her weary musings.

"Oh, she's fine," Amanda said quickly. "With the Bannons this season."

"The Bahamas." Marguerite sighed. "Those lovely straw hats and musical accents and blistering white beaches. I wish I were there now."

"Why not go?" Terry asked.

"Because the first time Mrs. Brown was fussy about Jason missing breakfast, he'd fire her," came the tight reply, "and this is the only time I've ever been able to keep a cook longer than three months. I'm standing guard over this one."

Terry looked out the back window uncomfortably. "He sounds a little hard to please." He laughed nervously.

"It depends on the mood he's in," Marguerite said. "Jason can be very kind. He's always easy to get along with when he's asleep. The only time we have problems is when he's awake."

Amanda laughed. "You'll scare Terry to death."

"Don't worry, now," Marguerite promised. "Just make sure he hasn't been near the cattle when you approach him, Terry." She frowned slightly. "Let's see, Sunday evenings are fairly safe, if nothing's broken down or if…"

"We'll talk to Duncan first," Amanda promised her colleague. "He doesn't bite."

"He doesn't always have Tess underfoot, either," Marguerite said in a faintly goaded tone.

"Maybe Jace will relent and marry her someday," Amanda suggested.

The older woman sighed. "I had hoped that you might be my daughter-in-law one day, Amanda."

"Be grateful for small blessings," came the smiling reply. "Duncan and I together would have driven you crazy."

"I wasn't thinking about my youngest," Marguerite said with frightening candor, and the look she gave Amanda made her pulse race.

She looked away. "Jace won't ever forgive me for that bull."

"It was unavoidable. You didn't ask the silly bull to crash through the fence."

"Jace was so angry," she recalled, shuddering. "I thought he was going to hit me."

"I always thought he was angry for a quite different reason. Oh, damn," Marguerite added with perfect enunciation when they turned into the long paved driveway that led to Casa Verde. "That's Tess's car," she grumbled.

Amanda saw it, a little Ferrari parked in the circular space that curved around the fishpond and fountain in front of the two-storey mansion.

"At least you know where Jace is," Amanda said lightly, although her pulse was doing double time.

"Yes, but I knew where he was when Gypsy was alive, and I liked Gypsy," Marguerite said stubbornly.

"Who was Gypsy?" Terry asked the two women, who both had burst into laughter.

"Jace's dog," Amanda volunteered through her giggles.

Marguerite pulled up behind the small black car and cut the engine. The house was over a century old, but still solid and welcoming, retaining its homey atmosphere. To Amanda, who loved it and remembered it from childhood, it wasn't a mansion or even a landmark. It was simply Duncan's house.

"Duncan and I used to hang by our heels from those low limbs on the oak tree at the corner of the house," Amanda told Terry as they walked up the azalea-lined path that led to the porch steps. "Duncan slipped and fell one day, and if Jace hadn't caught him, his head would have been half its present size."

"I shudder to think what might have happened," Marguerite said and her patrician face went rigid. "You and Duncan were always restless, my dear. Duncan has the wanderlust still. It's Jace who's put down strong roots."

Amanda's fingers tightened on her purse. She didn't like to think about Jace at all, but looking around that familiar porch brought back a bouquet of memories. And not all of them were pleasant.

"Your son said that we could take a look at the property tomorrow," Terry remarked casually. "I thought I might spend this evening filling his brother in on the way we handle our accounts."

"If you can get Jace to sit still long enough." Marguerite laughed. "Ask Amanda, she'll tell you how busy he is. I have to follow him around to ask him anything."

"At least I can ride." Terry laughed. "I suppose I could gallop along after him."

"Not the way Jace rides," Amanda said quietly.

Marguerite opened the front door and led her two guests inside the house. The entrance featured a highly polished heart of pine floor with an Oriental rug done in a predominantly red color scheme, and a marble-top table on which was placed an arrangement of elegant cut red roses from the massive rose garden that flanked the oval swimming pool behind the house.

A massive staircase with a red carpet protecting the steps led up to the second floor, and the dark oak bannister was smooth as glass with age and handling. The house gave Amanda goose pimples when she remembered some of the Westerners who were rumored to have enjoyed its hospitality. Legend had it that Uncle John Chisolm had once slept within its walls. The house had been restored, of course, and enlarged, but that bannister was the original one.

A maid came forward to take Amanda's lightweight sweater, followed by a man who relieved Terry of the suitcases.

"Diego and Maria." Marguerite introduced them only to Terry, because Amanda had recognized them. "The Lopezes. They're our mainstays. Without them we'd be helpless."

The mainstays grinned, bowed and went about making sure that the family wasn't left helpless.

"We'll have coffee and talk for a while," Marguerite said, leading them into the huge, white-carpeted living room with its royal blue furniture and curtains, its antique oak tables and upholstered chairs. "Isn't white ridiculous for a ranch carpet?" She laughed apologetically. "But even though I have to keep on replacing it, I can't resist this color scheme. Do sit down while I let Maria know we'll have our coffee in here. Jace must be down at the stables."

"No, he isn't," came a husky, bored voice from behind them in the hall, and Tess Anderson strolled into the room with her hands rammed deep in the pockets of her aqua knit skirt. Wearing a matching V-necked top, she looked like something out of a fashion show. Her black hair was loose and curling around her ears, her dark eyes snapping, her olive complexion absolutely stunning against the blood red lipstick she wore.

"Wow," Terry managed in a bare whisper, his eyes bulging at the vision in the doorway.

Tess accepted the male adulation as her due, gazing at Terry's thin, lackluster person dismissively. Her sharp eyes darted to Amanda, and she eyed the other girl's smart but businesslike suit with distaste.

"Jace is out looking at a new harvester with Bill Johnson," Tess said casually. "The old one they use on the bottoms broke down this morning."

"Bogged down in the hay, I reckon," Marguerite joked, knowing full well there wasn't enough moisture to bog anything down. "Has he stopped swearing yet?"

Tess didn't smile. "Naturally, it disturbed him. It's a very expensive piece of equipment. He asked me to stop by and tell you he'd be late."

"When has he ever been on time for a meal?" Marguerite asked curtly.

Tess turned away. "I've got to rush. Dad's waiting for me. Some business about selling one of the developments." She glanced back at Terry and Amanda. "I hear Duncan is thinking about hiring your agency to handle our Florida project. Dad and I want to be in on any discussions you have, naturally, since we do have a rather large sum invested."

"Of course," Terry said, reddening.

"We'll be in touch. 'Night, Marguerite," she called back carelessly. Her high heels beat a quick tattoo on the wood floor. Then the door slammed shut behind her and there was a conspicuous silence in the room.

Marguerite's dark eyes flashed fire. "And when did I give her permission to call me by my first name?"

Terry looked down at his shoes. "Snags," he murmured. "I should have known it seemed too easy."

"Don't fret," Amanda said cheerfully. "Mr. Anderson isn't at all like his daughter."

Terry brightened a little, but Marguerite was still muttering to herself as she left the room to tell Maria to bring coffee to the living room.

Maria brought the coffee on an enormous silver tray with an antique silver service and thin bone china cups in a burgundy and white pattern.

While Marguerite poured, Amanda studied the contents of the elegant display case against one wall. Inside, it was like a miniature museum of Western history. There was a .44 Navy Colt, a worn gunbelt that Jace's great uncle had worn on trail drives, a Comanche knife in an aging buckskin sheath decorated with faded beads, some of which were missing, and other mementos of an age long past. There was an old family Bible that Jace's people had brought all the way from Georgia by wagon train, and a Confederate pistol and officer's hat. There was even a peace pipe.

"Never get tired of looking at it, do you?" Marguerite asked gently.

She turned with a smile. "Not ever."

"Your people had a proud history, too," Marguerite said. "Did you manage to hold on to any of those French chairs and silver?"

Amanda shook her head. "Only the small things, I'm afraid." She sighed, feeling a great sense of loss. "There simply wasn't any place to keep them, except in storage, and they were worth so much money…it took quite a lot to pay the bills," she added sorrowfully.

Terry caught the look on her face and turned to Marguerite. "Tell me about the house," he said, frowning interestedly.

That caught the older woman's attention immediately, and an hour later she was still reciting tidbits from the past.

Amanda had been lulled into a sense of security, listening to her, and there was a quiet, wistful smile on her lovely face when the front door suddenly swung open. As she looked toward the doorway, she found her eyes caught and held by a pair almost the exact color of the antique silver service. Jace!

Chapter Three

Jason Everett Whitehall was the image of his late father. Tall and powerful, with eyes like polished silver in a darkly tanned face and a shock of coal-black hair, he would have drawn eyes anywhere. The patterned Western shirt he was wearing emphasized his broad shoulders just as the well-cut denim jeans hugged the lines of his muscular thighs and narrow hips. His expensive leather boots were dusty, but obviously meant for dress. The only disreputable note in his outfit was the worn black Stetson he held in his hand, just as battered now as it had been on Amanda's last unforgettable visit.

She couldn't drag her eyes away from him. They traced the hard lines of his face involuntarily, and she wondered now, as she had in her adolescence, if there was a trace of emotion in him. He seemed so completely removed from warmth or passion.

He was pleasant enough to Terry as he entered the room, shaking hands, making brief, polite work of the greetings.

"You know my junior partner, of course." Terry grinned, gesturing toward Amanda on the sofa beside him.

"I know her," Jace said in his deep, slow drawl, shooting her a hard glance that barely touched the slender curves of her body, curves that were only emphasized by the classical cut of her navy blue suit.

"We're not going to have much time to talk tonight," he told Terry without preamble. "I've got a long-standing date. But Duncan should be back tomorrow, and I'll try to find a few minutes later in the week to go over the whole proposal with you. You can give me the basics over supper."

"Fine!" Terry said. He was immediately charming and pleasant, and Amanda couldn't repress an amused smile, watching him. He was so obvious when he was trying to curry favor.

"How's your mother?" Jace asked Amanda curtly as he went to the bar to pour drinks.

Amanda felt her spine going rigid. "Very well, thanks," she said.

"Who is she imposing on this month?" he continued casually.

"Jason!" Marguerite burst out, horrified. She turned to her guests. "Amanda, wouldn't you like to freshen up? And, Terry, if you'll come along, I'll show you to your room at the same time." She herded them out of the room quickly, shooting a furious glance at her impassive son on the way.

"I don't know what in the world's wrong with him," Marguerite grumbled when she and Amanda were alone in the deliciously feminine blue wallpapered guest room. The pretty quilted blue bedspread was complemented by ruffled pillow shams and green plants grew lushly in attractive brass planters.

"He's just being himself," Amanda said with more humor than she felt. The words had hurt, as Jace meant them to. "I can't remember a time in my life when he hasn't cut at me."

Marguerite looked into the warm brown eyes and smiled, too. "That's my girl. Just ignore him."

"Oh, how can I?" Amanda asked, dramatically batting her long eyelashes. "He's so devastating, so masculine, so…manly."

Marguerite giggled like a young girl. She sat down on the edge of the thick quilted coverlet on the bed and folded her hands primly in her lap while Amanda hung up her few, painstakingly chosen business clothes. "You're the only woman I know who doesn't chase him mercilessly," she pointed out. "He's considered quite a catch, you know."

"If I caught him, I'd throw him right back," Amanda said, unruffled. "He's too aggressively masculine to suit me, too domineering. I'm a little afraid of him, I think," she admitted honestly.

"Yes, I know," the older woman replied kindly.

"Tess isn't, though." She sighed. "Maybe they deserve each other," she added with a mean laugh.

"Tess! If he marries that girl, I will move to Australia and set up housekeeping in an opal mine!" Marguerite threatened.

"That bad?"

"My dear, the last time she helped Jace with a sale, she had Maria in tears and one of my daily maids quit without notice on the spot. As you saw today, she simply takes over, and Jace does nothing to stop her."

"It is your house," Amanda reminded her gently.

The thin shoulders rose and fell expressively. "I used to think so. Lately she's talked about remodeling my kitchen."

Amanda toyed with a button on one of the simple tailored blouses she was hanging in the closet. "Are they engaged?"

"I don't know. Jace tells me nothing. I suppose if he decides to marry her, the first I'll hear of it will be on the evening news!"

Amanda laughed softly. "I can't imagine Jace married."

"I can't imagine Jace the way he's been, period." Marguerite stood up. "For months now he's walked around scowling, half-hearing me, so busy I can't get two words out of him. And even Tess—you know, sometimes I get the very definite impression that Tess is like a fly to him, but he's just too busy to swat her."

Amanda burst out laughing. The thought of the decorative brunette as a fly was totally incongruous. Tess, with her perfect makeup, flawless coiffures, and designer fashions would be horrified to hear them discussing her like this.

Marguerite smiled. "I'm glad you don't take what Jace says to heart. Your mother is my best friend, and none of what he said is true."

"But it is," Amanda protested quietly. "We both know it, too. Mother is still living in the past. She won't accept things the way they are."

"That's still no excuse for Jace to ridicule her," Marguerite replied. "I'm going to have a talk with him about that."

"If the way he looked at me was anything to go by, I think I'd feed him and get him drunk before I did that," Amanda suggested.

"I've never seen him drunk," came the soft reply. "Although, he came close to it once," she added, throwing a pointed look at the younger woman before she turned away. "I'll see you downstairs. Don't feel that you have to change, or dress up. We're still very informal."

That was a blessing, Amanda thought later when she looked at her meager wardrobe. At one time, it would have boasted designer labels and fine silks and organzas with hand-embroidered hems. Now she had to limit spending to the necessities. With careful shopping and her own innate good taste, she had put together an attractive, if limited, wardrobe, concentrating on the clothes she needed for work. There wasn't an evening gown in the lot. Oh, well, at least she wouldn't need one of those.

She showered and slipped into a white pleated skirt with a pretty navy blue blouse and tied a white ruffled scarf at her throat to complete the simple but attractive-looking outfit. She tied her hair back with a piece of white ribbon, and slipped her hosed feet into a pair of dark blue sandals. Then with a quick spray of cologne and a touch of lipstick, she went downstairs.

Terry was the first person she saw, standing in the doorway of the living room with a brandy snifter in his hand.

"There you are." He grinned, his eyes sweeping up and down her slender figure mischievously. "Going sailing?"

"Thought I might," she returned lightly. "Care to swim alongside and fend off the sharks?"

He shook his head. "I suffer from acute cowardice,

brought on by proximity to sharks. One of them was rumored to have eaten a great-aunt of mine."

With a laugh like sunlight filtering into a yellow room, she walked past him into the spacious living room and found herself looking straight into Jace's silvery eyes. That intense stare of his was disconcerting, and it did crazy things to her heart. She jerked her own gaze down to the carpet.

"Would you like some sherry?" he asked her tightly.

She shook her head, moving to Terry's side like a kitten edging up to a tomcat for safety. "No, thanks."

Terry put a thin arm around her shoulders affectionately. "She's a caffeine addict," he told Jace. "She doesn't drink."

Jace looked as if he wanted to crush his brandy snifter in his powerful brown fingers and grind it into the carpet. Amanda couldn't remember ever seeing that particular look on his face before.

He turned away before she had time to analyze it. "Let's go in. Mother will be down eventually." He led the way into the dining room, and Amanda couldn't help admire the fit of his brown suit with its attractive Western yoke, the way it emphasized his broad shoulders from the back. He was an attractive man. Too attractive.

Amanda was disconcerted to find herself seated close beside Jace, so close that her foot brushed his shiny brown leather boot under the table. She drew it back quickly, aware of his taut, irritated glance.

"Tell me why Duncan thinks we need an advertising agency," Jace invited arrogantly, leaning back in his chair so that the buttons of his white silk shirt strained against the powerful muscles of his chest. The shirt was open at the throat, and there were shadows under its thinness, hint-ing at the covering of thick, dark hair over the bronzed flesh. Amanda remembered without wanting to how Jace looked without a shirt. She drew her eyes back to her spotless china plate as Mrs. Brown, Marguerite's prize cook, ambled in with dishes of expertly prepared food. A dish containing thick chunks of breaded, fried cube steak and a big steaming bowl of thick milk gravy were set on the spotless white linen tablecloth, along with a platter of cat's head biscuits, real butter, cabbage, a salad, asparagus tips in hollandaise sauce, a creamy fruit salad, homemade rolls and cottage fried potatoes. Amanda couldn't remember when she'd been confronted by such a lavish selection of dishes, and she realized with a start how long it had been since she'd been able to afford to set a table like this.

She nibbled at each delicious spoonful as if it would be her last, savoring every bite, while Terry's pleasant voice rambled on.

Marguerite joined them in the middle of Terry's sales pitch, smiling all around as she sat in her accustomed place at the elegant table with its centerpiece of white daisies.

"I'm sorry to be late," she said, "but I lost track of time. There's a mystery theater on the local radio station, and I'm just hooked on it."

"Detective stories," Jace scoffed. "No wonder you leave your light on at night."

Marguerite lifted her thin face proudly. "A lot of people use night-lights."

"You use three lamps," he commented. His gray eyes sparkled at her and he winked suddenly, smiling. Amanda, on the fringe of that smile, felt something warm kindle inside her. He was devastating when he used that inherent charm of his. No woman alive could have resisted it, but she'd only seen it once, a very long time ago. She dropped her eyes back to her plate and finished the last of her fruit salad with a sigh.

In the middle of Terry's wrap-up, the phone rang and, seconds later, Jace was called away from the table.

Marguerite glared after him. "Once," she muttered, "just once, to have an uninterrupted meal! If it isn't some problem with the ranch that Bill Johnson, our manager, can't handle, it's a personnel problem at one of the companies, or some salesman wanting to interest him in a new tractor, or another rancher trying to sell him a bull, or a newspaper wanting information on a merger." She glared into space. "Last week it was a magazine wanting to know if Jace was getting married. I told them yes," she said with ill-concealed irritation, "and I can't wait until someone shoves the article under his nose!"

Amanda laughed until tears ran down her cheeks. "Oh, how could you?"

"How could she what?" Jace asked, returning just in time to catch that last remark.

Amanda shook her head, dabbing at her eyes with her linen napkin while Marguerite's thin face seemed to puff up indignantly.

"Another disaster?" Marguerite asked him as he sat back down. "The world goes to war if you finish one meal?"

Jace raised an eyebrow at her, sipping his coffee. "Would you like to take over?"

"I'd simply love it," she told her son. "I'd sell everything."

"And condemn Duncan and me to growing roses?" he teased.

She relented. “Well if we could just have one whole meal together, Jason…”

“How would you cope?” he teased. “It’s never happened.”

“And when your father was still alive, it was worse,” she admitted. She laughed. “I remember throwing his plate at him once when he went to talk to an attorney during dinner on Christmas Day.”

Jace smiled mockingly. “I remember what happened when he came back,” he reminded her, and Marguerite Whitehall blushed like a schoolgirl.

“Oh, by the way,” Marguerite began, “I—”

Before she could get the words out, Maria came in to announce that Tess was on the phone and wanted to speak to Jace.

Marguerite glared at him as he passed her on his way to the hall phone a second time. “Why don’t you have a special phone invented with a plate attached?” she asked nastily. “Or better, an edible phone, so you could eat and talk at the same time?”

Amanda’s solemn face dissolved into laughter. It had been this way with the Whitehalls forever. Marguerite had had this same argument with Jude.

The older woman shook her head, glancing toward Terry with a mischievous smile. “Would you like to explain the advertising business to me, Terry? I can’t give you the account, but I won’t rush off in the middle of your explanation to answer the phone.”

Terry laughed, lifting a homemade roll to his mouth. “No problem, Mrs. Whitehall. There’s plenty of time. We’ll be here a week, after all.”

During which, Amanda was thinking, you might get Jace to yourself for ten minutes. But she didn’t say it.

Later, everyone seemed to vanish. Jace went upstairs, and Marguerite carried Terry off to show him her collection of jade figurines, leaving Amanda alone in the living room.

She finished her after-dinner cup of coffee and put the saucer gingerly back down on the coffee table. Perhaps, she thought wildly, it might be a good idea to go up to her room. If Jace came downstairs before the others got back, she'd be stuck with him, and she didn't want that headache. Being alone with Jace was one circumstance she'd never be prepared for.

She hurried out into the hall, but before she even made it to the staircase, she saw Jace coming down it. He'd added a brown-and-gold tie to the white silk shirt and brown suit, and he looked maddeningly elegant.

"Running?" he asked pointedly, his eyes narrow and cold as they studied her.

Chapter Four

She froze in the center of the entrance, staring at him helplessly. He made her nervous. He always had.

"I…was just going up to my room for a minute," she faltered.

He came the rest of the way down without hesitation, his booted feet making soft thuds on the carpeted steps. He paused in front of her when he got to the bottom, towering over her, close enough that she could smell his woodsy cologne and the clean fragrance of his body.

"For what?" he asked with a mocking smile. "A handkerchief?"

"More like a shield and some armor," she countered, hiding her nervousness behind humor.

He didn't laugh. "You haven't changed," he observed. "Still the little clown." His narrowed eyes slid down her body indifferently. "Why did you come back here?" he demanded abruptly, cold steel in his tone.

"Because Duncan insisted."

He scowled down at her. "Why? You only work for Black."

"I'm his partner," she replied. "Didn't you know?"

He stared at her intently. "How did you manage that?" he asked contemptuously. "Or do I need to ask?"

She saw what he was driving at and her face flamed. "It isn't like that," she said tightly.

"Isn't it?" He glared at her. "At least I offered you more than a share in a third-class business."

Her face went a fiery red. "That's all women are to you," she accused. "Toys, sitting on a shelf waiting to be bought."

"Tess isn't," he said with deliberate cruelty.

"How lovely for her," she threw back.

He stuck his hands in his pockets and looked down his arrogant nose at her. There was a strange, foreign something behind those glittering eyes that disturbed her.

"You're thinner," he remarked.

She shrugged. "I work hard."

"Doing what?" he asked curtly. "Sleeping with the boss?"

"I don't!" she burst out. She looked up into his dark face, her own pale in the blazing light of the crystal chandelier. "Why do you hate me so? Was the bull so important?"

His face seemed to set even harder. "A grand champion, and you can ask that? My God, you didn't even apologize!"

"Would it have brought him back?" she asked sadly.

"No." A muscle in his jaw moved.

"You won't…you won't let your dislike of me prejudice you against the agency, will you?" she asked suddenly.

"Afraid your boss might lose his shirt?" he taunted.

"Something like that."

He cocked his head down at her, his hard mouth set. "Why don't you tell me the truth? Duncan didn't invite you down here. You came on your own initiative." He smiled mockingly. "I haven't forgotten how you used to tag after him. And now you've got more reason than ever."

She saw red. All the years of backing away dissolved, and she felt suddenly reckless.

"You go to hell, Jace Whitehall," she said coldly, her brown eyes throwing off sparks as she lifted her angry face.

Both dark eyebrows went up over half astonished, half amused silver eyes. "What?"

But before she could repeat the dangerous words, Terry's voice broke in between them.

"Oh, there you are," he called cheerfully. "Come back in here and keep us company. It's too early to turn in."

Jace's eyes were hidden behind those narrowed eyelids, and he turned away before Amanda could puzzle out the new look in them.

"Off again?" Marguerite asked pleasantly. "Where are you taking Tess?"

"Out," he said noncommittally, reaching down to kiss the wrinkled pink cheek. "Good night."

He pivoted on his heel and left them without another word, closing the door firmly behind him.

Terry stared at Amanda. "Did I hear you say what I thought I heard you say?"

"My question exactly," Marguerite added.

Amanda stirred under their intent stares and went ahead of them into the living room. "Well, he deserved it," she muttered. "Arrogant, insulting beast!"

Marguerite laughed delightedly, a mysterious light in her eyes that she was careful to conceal.

"What is it with you two?" Terry asked her. "If ever I saw mutual dislike…"

"My mother once called Jace a cowboy," Amanda replied. "It was a bad time to do it, and she was terribly insulting, and Jace never got over it."

"Jace took to calling Amanda 'lady,'" Marguerite continued. She smiled at the younger woman. "She was, and is, that. But Jace meant it in another sense."

"As in Lady MacBeth," Amanda said. Her eyes clouded. "I'd like to cook him a nice mess of buttered toadstools," she said with a malicious smile.

"Down, girl," Terry said. "Vinegar catches no flies."

Amanda remembered what Marguerite had said about Tess, and when their eyes met, she knew the older woman was also remembering. They both burst into laughter, dissolving the sombre mood memory had brought to cloud the evening.

But later that night, alone in her bedroom, memories returned to haunt her. Seeing Jace again had resurrected all the old scars, and she felt the pain of them right through her slender body. Her eyes wide open, staring at the strange patterns the moonlight made on the ceiling of her room, she drifted back to that Friday seven years ago when she'd gone running along the fence that separated her father's pasture from the Whitehalls' property, laughing as she jumped on the lower rung of the fence and watched Jace slow his big black stallion and canter over to her.

"Looking for Duncan?" he'd asked curtly, his eyes angry in that cold, hard face that never seemed to soften.

"No, for you," she'd corrected, glancing at him shyly.

"I'm having a party tomorrow night. I'll be sixteen, you know."

He'd stared at her with a strangeness about him that still puzzled her years later, his eyes giving nothing away as they glittered over her slender body, her flushed, exuberant face. She'd never felt more alive than she did that day, and Jace couldn't know that it had taken her the better part of the morning to get up enough nerve to seek him out. Duncan was easy to talk to. Jace was something else. He fascinated her, even as he frightened her. Already a man even then, he had a blatant sensuousness that made her developing emotions run riot.

"Well, what do you want me to do about it?" he'd asked coldly.

The vibrant laughter left her face, draining away, and some of her nerve had gone with it. "I, uh…I wanted to invite you to my party," she choked.

He studied her narrowly over the cigarette he put between his chiseled lips and lit. "And what did your mother think about that idea?"

"She said it was fine with her," she returned rebelliously, omitting how hard she'd had to fight Bea to make the invitation to the Whitehall brothers.

"Like hell," Jace had replied knowingly.

She'd tossed her silver-blond hair, risking her pride. "Will you come, Jason?" she'd asked quietly.

"Just me? Aren't you inviting Duncan as well?"

"Both of you, of course, but Duncan said you wouldn't come unless I asked you," she replied truthfully.

He'd drawn a deep, hard breath, blowing out a cloud of smoke with it. His eyes had been thoughtful on her young, hopeful face.

"Will you, Jace?" she'd persisted meekly.

"Maybe," was as far as he'd commit himself. He'd wheeled the horse without another word, leaving her to stare after him in a hopeless, disappointed daze.

The amazing thing was that Jace had come to the party with Duncan, dressed in immaculately stylish dark evening clothes. He looked like a fashion plate, and, to Amanda's sorrow, he was neatly surrounded by admiring teenage girls before he was through the door. Most of her girlfriends were absolutely beautiful young debutantes, very sophisticated and worldly. Not at all like young Amanda, who was painfully shy and unworldly, standing quietly in the corner with her blond hair piled on top of her head. Her exposed throat looked vulnerable, her pink lips soft, and her brown eyes stared wistfully at Jace despite the fact that Duncan spent the evening dancing attendance on her. She'd looked down at her green-embroidered white organdy dress in disgust, hating it. The demure neckline, puffed sleeves and full, flowing skirt hadn't been exciting enough to catch and hold Jace's eye. Of course, she'd told herself, Jace was twenty-five to her sixteen, and probably wouldn't have been caught dead looking at a girl her age. But her heart had ached to have him notice her. She'd danced woodenly with Duncan and the other boys, her eyes following Jace everywhere. She'd longed to dance just one dance with him.

It had been the last dance, a slow tune about lost love that Amanda had thought quite appropriate at the time. Jace hadn't asked her to dance. He'd held out his hand, and she'd put hers into it, feeling it swallow her fingers warmly. Even the way he danced had been exciting. He'd held her young body against his by keeping both hands at her waist, leaving her hands to rest on his chest while they moved lazily to the music. She could still smell the expensive oriental cologne he'd been wearing, feel the warmth of his tall, athletic body against the length of hers as they moved, sense the hard, powerful muscles of his thighs pressed close to her even through the layers of material that made up her skirt. Her heart had gone wild in her chest at the proximity. New, frightening emotions had drained her, made her weak in his supporting arms. She'd looked up at him with all her untried longings plain in her eyes, and he'd stopped dancing abruptly and, catching her hand, had led her out onto the dark patio overlooking the night lights of Victoria.

"Is this what you want, honey?" he'd asked, crushing her against him with a curious anger in his voice. "To see how I rate as a lover?"

"Jace, I didn't—" she began to protest.

But even as she opened her mouth to speak, his lips had crushed down on it, rough and uncompromising, deliberately cruel. His arms had riveted her to the length of him, bruising her softness in a silence that had combined the distant strains of music with the night sounds of crickets and frogs, and the harsh sigh of Jace's breath with the rustle of clothing as he caught her ever closer. His teeth had nipped her lip painfully, making her moan with fright, as he subjected her to her first kiss and taught her the dangers of flirting with an experienced man. With a wrenching fear, she'd felt his big, warm hand sliding up from her waist to the soft, high curve of her breast, breaking all the rules she'd been taught as he touched and savored the rounded softness of her body.

"It's like touching silk," he'd murmured against her

mouth, drawing back slightly to stare down at her. "Look at me," he'd said gruffly. "Let me see your face."

She'd raised frightened eyes to his, pushing at his hand in a flurry of outrage and embarrassment. "Don't," she'd whispered.

"Why not?" His eyes had glittered, going down to the darkness of his fingers against the white organdy of her bodice. "Isn't this why you asked me here tonight, Amanda? To see if a ranch hand makes love like a gentleman?"

She'd torn out of his arms, tears of humiliation glistening in her eyes.

"Don't you like the truth?" he'd asked, and he laughed at her while he lit a cigarette with steady fingers. "Sorry to disappoint you, little girl, but I've gone past ranch hand now. I'm the boss. I've not only paid off Casa Verde, I'm going to make a legend of it. I'm going to have the biggest damned spread in Texas before I'm through. And then, if I'm still tempted, I might give you another try." His eyes had hurt as they studied her like a side of beef. "You'll have to round out a bit more, though. You're too thin."

She hadn't been able to find the right words, and Duncan had appeared to rescue her before she had to. She'd never invited Jace to another party, though, and she'd gone to great lengths to stay out of his way. That hadn't bothered him a bit. She often suspected that he really did hate her.

That night, Amanda slept fitfully, her dreams disturbed by scenes she couldn't remember when she woke up early the next morning. She dragged herself out of bed and pulled on the worn blue terry-cloth robe at the foot of her bed, her long blond hair streaming down her back and over her shoulders in a beautiful silver-blond tangle that only made her look prettier. She huddled in the robe in the chill morning air that blew the curtains back from the window. She'd opened it last night so that she could drink in the fresh clean country air.

A knock at the door brought her to her feet again from her perch on the vanity bench, and she yawned as she padded barefoot to the door. Her eyes fell sadly to the old robe, remembering satin ones she used to own that had dainty little fur scuffs to match. Her shoulders shrugged. That life was over. It was just a dream, washed away by the riptide of reality.

She opened the door, expecting Maria, and found Duncan grinning down at her, brown-eyed and boyish.

"Good morning, ma'am," he said merrily.

"Duncan!" she cried, and, careless of convention, threw herself into his husky arms. They closed around her warmly and she caught the familiar scent of the spice cologne he'd always worn.

"Missed me, did you?" he asked at her ear, because he was only a couple of inches taller than she was—not at all as towering and formidable as Jace. "Not even a postcard in six months, either."

"I didn't think you'd want to hear from me," she murmured.

"Why not? It wasn't my bull you ran over." He chuckled.

"No, it was mine," came a rough voice from behind Duncan, and Amanda stiffened involuntarily.

Tugging away from Duncan, she shook back her wealth of soft, curling hair and glared at Jace's set face. He was dressed for work this morning, in expensively cut but faded jeans and a gray shirt that just matched his cold, narrow eyes. Atop his head was the old black Stetson.

"Good morning, Jace," she said with chilling sweetness. "So sorry I forgot my manners yesterday. I haven't thanked you for your warm reception."

Jace threw up an eyebrow, and there was something indefinable in the look he gave her. "Don't strain yourself, Lady."

Her face burned. "My name is Amanda. Or Miss Carson. Or hey, you. But don't call me Lady. I don't like it."

One corner of Jace's hard mouth went up in a taunting smile. "Brave in company, aren't you? Try it when we're alone."

"Make sure your insurance is paid up first, won't you?" she said, smiling venomously.

"Now, friends," Duncan interrupted, "this is no way to start off a beautiful morning. Especially when we haven't even had breakfast."

"Haven't we?" Amanda asked. "Your brother's had two bites of me already."

Jace cocked his head at her and his eyes sparkled dangerously, like sun on ice crystals. "Careful, honey. I hit back."

"Go ahead," she challenged bravely.

"On my own ground," he said with the light of battle kindling in his face. "And in my own time." He looked from Amanda to Duncan. "What came out of the meeting?"

"Jenkins is interested," the younger man replied with a smile. "I think I hooked him. We'll know tomorrow. Meanwhile, has Black explained what the ad agency can do for us on that Florida development?"

"Briefly, but not in any detail," Jace replied.

"What do you think?" Duncan persisted, his brown eyes questioning Jace's gray ones.

Jace stared back. "I'll have to hear more about it. A hell of a lot more."

"Sounds like we're in for a long week." The younger man sighed.

"It may be too long for some of us," came the curt reply, and a pair of silvery eyes cut at Amanda. "And if Lady here doesn't get that chip off her shoulder, Black can damned well take his proposal back to San Antonio without my signature on any contract."

Amanda hated him for that threat. It was all the more despicable because she knew he meant it. He'd carry his resentment of her over into business, and he was ruthless enough to deny Terry the account out of sheer spite. Jace never bluffed. He never had to. People always came around to his way of thinking in the end.

"Now, Jace," Duncan began, mediating as always.

"I've got work to do," Jace growled, pivoting on his booted heel. "Come on down to the Kennedy bottoms when you've had breakfast and I'll show you the young bull I bought at the Western Heritage sale last week."

"Can I bring Amanda?" Duncan asked with calculating eyes.

Jace's broad shoulders stiffened. He glanced back angrily. "I'd like to keep this one," he said curtly, and kept walking.

Amanda's face froze. She glared at the long, muscular back with pure hatred. "I wish he'd fall down the stairs," she muttered.

"Jace never falls," he reminded her. "And if he ever did, he'd land on his feet." He grinned down at her. "My, my, how you've changed. You never used to talk back to him."

"I'm twenty-three years old, and he's not using me for a doormat anymore," she replied with cool hauteur.

Duncan nodded, and she thought she detected a hint of smugness in his eyes before they darted away. "Get dressed and come on down," he told her. "I'm anxious to hear about the ad campaign you and Black have worked up."

"Do Tess and her father have to see it, too?" she asked suddenly.

"Tess!" he grumbled. "I'd forgotten about her. Well, we'll cross that bridge later. Jace and I have a bigger investment than the Andersons, so we'll have the final say."

"Jace will side with them," she said certainly.

"He might surprise you. In fact," he added mysteriously, "I'd bet on it. Get dressed, girl, time's a-wasting!"

She saluted him. "Yes, sir!"

Later in the day, Duncan took his guests out for a ride around the ranch on horseback, taking care to see that Terry—an admitted novice—got a slow, gentle mount.

The ranch stretched off in every direction, fenced in green and white, with neat barns and even neater paddocks. It was a staggering operation.

"Jace's computer stores records on over a hundred thousand head," Duncan told Terry as they watched the beefy Santa Gertrudis cattle graze, their rich red coats burning in the sun. "We're fortunate enough to be able to run both purebred and grade cattle here, and we have our own feedlot. We don't have to contract our beef cattle out before we sell them. We can feed them out right here on the ranch."

Terry blinked. Ranch talk was new to him, but to Amanda, who knew and loved every stick and horn on the place, it was familiar and interesting.

"Remember how that old Brahma bull of your father's used to chase the dogs?" Amanda asked Duncan wistfully.

He nodded. "Mother always threatened to sell him for beef after he killed her spaniel. When Dad died, she did exactly that," he added with a shake of his head. "Over a hundred thousand dollars worth of prime beef. We actually ate him. A vindictive woman, my mother."

"Didn't Jace try to stop her?" Amanda asked incredulously.

"Jace didn't know about it." He chuckled. "Mother dared me to open my mouth. And he was off the property so much checking on the other ranches, he didn't notice the animal was missing."

"What did he do when he found out?"

"Threw back his head and laughed," Duncan told her.

Both eyebrows went up. "All that money…!"

"Strange how different Jace is with you," he remarked. "He's the easiest man in the world to get along with, as far as the rest of us are concerned."

Amanda turned away from those probing eyes and looked out across the range. "Did you mention something about showing us the new bull?" she hedged.

"Sure. Follow me." Duncan grinned.

It was roundup at its best, and hundreds of calves were being vetted in a chuted corral with gates opening into paddocks on all four sides. In the midst of the noise, bawling cattle, dust, yelling cowboys and blazing sun was Jace Whitehall, straddling the fence, overseeing the whole operation. His interest in ranch work had never waned, even though he could have gone the rest of his life without ever donning jeans and a work hat again. He was rich now, successful, and his financial wizardry had placed him in a luxurious office in a skyscraper in downtown Victoria. He didn't have to work cattle. In fact, for a man in his position, it was unusual that he did. But then Jace was unconventional. And Amanda wondered if he hadn't really enjoyed ranch work more before it made him wealthy. He was an outdoor man at heart, not a desk-bound executive.

He caught sight of Amanda at once, and even at a distance, she could feel the ferocity of his look. But she straightened proudly and schooled her delicate features to calmness. It wouldn't do to let Jace know how he really affected her.

"Don't let him rattle you, Mandy," Duncan said under his breath. "He picks at you out of pure habit, not malice. He doesn't really mean anything."

"He's not walking all over me anymore," she returned stubbornly. "Whether or not he means it."

"Declaring war?" he teased.

"With all batteries blazing," she returned. She put up a hand to push a loose strand of her silvery hair back in place.

"I came to see the calves," Duncan called to his brother.

Jace leaped gracefully down from the fence and walked toward them, pausing to tear off his hat and wipe his sweaty brow on the sleeve of his dusty shirt. "Did you need to bring a delegation?" he asked, staring pointedly at Amanda and Terry.

"We did think about hiring a bus and bringing the kitchen staff," Amanda agreed with a bold smile.

Jace's glittering silver eyes narrowed. "Why don't you come down here and get cute," he invited curtly.

"Grass allergy," she murmured. "Dust, too. Horrible to watch."

Duncan chuckled. "Incorrigible child," he teased.

"How do you stand the dust and the heat?" Terry asked incredulously. "Not to mention the noise!"

"Long practice," Jace told him. "And necessity. It isn't easy work."

"I'll never complain about beef prices again," Terry promised, shading his eyes with his hand as he watched the men at work sorting and tagging and branding.

"Hi, Happy!" Amanda called to an old, grizzled cowboy who was just coming up behind Jace with his sweaty hat pushed back over his gray hair.

"Hello, Many!" the old cowboy greeted her with a toothless grin. "Come down to help us brand these little dogies?"

"Only if I get a nice, thick steak when you finish," she teased. Happy had been one of her father's foremen before…

"How's your mama?" Happy asked.

Amanda avoided Jace's mocking smile. "Fine, thanks."

Happy nodded. "Good to see you," he said, reading the hard look he was getting from Jace. "I'd better get back to work."

"Damned straight," Jace replied curtly, watching the older man move quickly away.

"It was my fault, Jace," Amanda said quietly. "I spoke to him first."

He ignored her soft plea. "Show Black the Arabians," he told his brother. "They're well worth the ride, if he thinks his anatomy will stand it," he added with an amused glance at Terry, who was standing up in the stirrups with a muffled groan.

"Thanks, I'd love to," Terry said through gritted teeth.

Jace chuckled, and just for a moment the hard lines left his face. "Don't push it," he advised the younger man. "It's going to be tough walking again as it is. Plenty of time."

Terry nodded. "Thanks," he said, and meant it this time. "I'll pass on the horses today."

"We'll head back, then," Duncan said, wheeling his mount. "Amanda, race you!" he called the challenge.

"Hold it!" Jace's voice rang out above the bawling cattle.

Amanda stopped so suddenly that she went forward in the saddle as a lean, powerful hand caught at the bridle of her mount and pulled him up short.

"No racing," Jace said curtly, daring her to argue with him as he averted his gaze to Duncan. "She's too accident-prone."

Duncan only looked amused. "If you say so."

"I'm not a child," Amanda protested, glaring down at the tall man.

He looked up into her eyes, and there was a look in his that held banked-down flames, puzzling, fascinating. She didn't look away, and something like an electric shock tore through her body.

Jace's firm jaw tautened and abruptly he released the reins and moved away. "If Summers calls me about that foundation sale, send somebody out to get me," he told Duncan, and then he was gone, striding back into the tangle of men and cattle without a backward glance.

Duncan didn't say a word, but there was an amused smile on his face when they headed back to the house, and Amanda was glad that Terry was too concerned with his aching muscles to pay much attention to what was going on around him. That look in Jace's eyes, even in memory, could jack up her heart rate. It wasn't contempt, or hatred. It was a fierce, barely contained hunger, and it terrified her to think that Jace felt that way. Ever since her disastrous sixteenth birthday party, she'd kept her distance from him. Now, finally, she was forced to admit the reason for it, if only to herself. Fastidious and cool, Amanda had never felt those raging fires that drove women to run after men. But she felt them when she looked at Jace. She always had, and it would be incredibly dangerous to let him know it. It would give him the most foolproof way to pay her back for all his imagined grievances, and she wouldn't be able to resist him. She'd know that for a long time, too.

She glanced back over her shoulder at the branding that was proceeding without a hitch in the corral. If Jace hadn't been there, Amanda would have loved to stay and watch the process. It was fascinating to see how the old hands worked the cattle. But Jace would have made her too nervous to enjoy it. She urged her mount into a trot and followed along behind the men.

Terry didn't move for the rest of the afternoon. He spread his spare body out in a lawn chair by the deep blue water of the oval swimming pool, under a leafy magnolia tree, and dozed. Amanda sat idly chatting with Duncan at the umbrella table, sipping her lemonade, comfortably dressed in an aged ankle-length aqua terry-cloth lounging dress with slit sides and white piping around the V-necked, sleeveless bodice. She could no longer afford to buy this sort of thing and the dress was left over from better days. Her feet were bare, and her hair was loose, lifting gently in the soft breeze. All around the pool area, there were blooming shrubs and masses of pink, white and red roses in the flower gardens that were Marguerite's pride and joy.

Her eyes wandered to the little gray summer house further along on the luscious green lawn, with its miniature split rail fence. It was a child's dream, and all the family's nieces and nephews and cousins had played there at one time or another.

"What do you really think of the campaign we've laid out?" Amanda asked Duncan.

"I like it," he said bluntly. "The question is, will Jace? He's not that keen on the real estate operation, but even so he's aware that it's going to take some work to sell the idea of an apartment complex in inland Florida. Most people want beachfront."

She nodded. "We can make it work with specialty advertising," she said quietly. "I'm sure of it."

Duncan smiled at her. "Are you the same girl who left here a few years ago, all nervous glances and shy smiles? Goodness, Miss Carson, you've changed. I noticed it six months ago, but there's an even bigger difference now."

"Am I really so different?" she mused.

"The way you stand up to Jace is different," he remarked dryly. "You've got him on his ear."

She flushed wildly. "It doesn't show."

"It does to me."

She looked up. "Why did you insist that I come with Terry?" she asked flatly.

"I'll tell you someday," he promised. "Right now I just want to sit and enjoy the sun."

"I think I'll go help Marguerite address invitations to her party." She rose, willowy and delightful in the long dress, her bare feet crushing the soft grass as she walked and her long hair tossing like silver floss in the breeze.

Duncan let out a long, leering whistle, and she smiled secretly to herself, pulling off her sunglasses as she walked, to tuck them into one of the two big pockets in the front of the dress.

She went around to the back entrance, where masses of white roses climbed on white trellises. Impulsively, she reached out to one of the fragrant blossoms just as a truck came careening around the house and braked at the back steps.

Jace swung out of the passenger seat, holding his arm where blood streamed down it through the thin blue patterned fabric.

"Go on back," Jace called to the driver. "I'll get Duncan to bring me down when I patch this up."

The driver nodded and wheeled the truck around, disappearing at the corner of the house.

Amanda stared dumbly at the blood. "You're hurt," she said incredulously, as if it was unthinkable.

"If you're going to faint, don't get between me and the door," he said curtly, moving forward.

She shook her head. "I won't faint. You'd better let me dress it for you. I don't think it would be very easy to manage one-handed."

"I've done it before," he replied, following her through the spotless kitchen and out into the hall that led to the downstairs bathroom.

"I don't doubt it a bit," she returned with a mischievous glance. "I can see you now, sewing up a gash on your back."

"You little brat," he growled.

"Don't insult me or I'll put the bandage on inside out." She led him into the bathroom and pulled out a vanity bench for him to sit on. He whipped off his hat and dropped it to the blue-and-white mosaic tile on the floor.

While she riffled through the cabinet for bandages and antiseptic, his eyes wandered over her slender body moving down the soft tangle of her long hair to the clinging aqua dress. "Water nymph," he murmured.

She looked down at him, shocked by the sensuous remark, and blushed involuntarily.

"What have you been doing, decorating my pool?" he asked when she turned back to run a basin of water and toss a soft clean cloth into it.

"I've been listening to Terry moan and beg for a quick and merciful end," she replied with a faint smile. "You'll have to take off your shirt," she added unnecessarily.

He flicked open the buttons with a lazy hand, his eyes intent on her profile. "Tess would be helping me," he remarked deliberately.

"Tess would be on the floor, unconscious," she retorted, refusing to be baited. His flirting puzzled her, frightened her. It was new and exciting and vaguely terrifying. "You know blood makes her sick."

He chuckled softly, easing his broad, powerful shoulders out of the blood-and-dust-stained garment, dropping it carelessly on the floor.

She turned with the washcloth held poised in her slender hand, her eyes drawn helplessly to the bronzed, muscular chest with its mat of curling black hair, to the rounded, hard muscles of his brown arms. She felt her heart doing acrobatics inside her chest, and hated her own reaction to him. He was so arrogantly, vibrantly male. Just looking at him made her weak, vulnerable.

His glittering silver eyes narrowed on her face. "You're staring," he said quietly.

"Sorry," she murmured inadequately, feeling her whole body stiffen as she leaned down to bathe the long, jagged gash above his elbow. "It's deep, Jace."

"I know. Just clean it, don't make unnecessary remarks," he bit off, tensing even at the light touch.

"It needs stitches," she said stubbornly.

"So did half a dozen other cuts, but I haven't died yet," he replied gruffly.

"I hope you've at least had a tetanus shot."

"You're joking, of course," he said tightly.

He was right. It was ridiculous to even think he wouldn't have had that much foresight. She finished cleaning the long gash and turned to get the can of antiseptic spray.

"Spray the cut, not the rest of me," he said, watching her shake the can and aim it.

"I ought to spray you with iodine," she told him irritatedly. "That," she added with an unkind smile, "would hurt."

He lifted his arrogant face and studied her narrowly. "You wouldn't like the way I'd get even."

She ignored the veiled threat and proceeded to wind clean white gauze around the arm. "I wish you'd see a doctor."

"If it starts to turn green from your amateurish efforts, I will," he promised.

Her eyes flashed down at him and found, instead of menace, laughter in his dark, hard face. "You make my blood burn, Jace Whitehall!" she muttered, rougher than she meant to be as she tied the bandage.

"Revealing words, Miss Carson," he said gently, and watched the color run into her cheeks.

"Not that way!" she protested without thinking.

Both dark eyebrows went up. "Oh?"

She turned and started to put away the bandages, refusing to look at him. It was too dangerous.

"From riches to rags," he commented, a lightning eye appraising the age of her aqua dress. "Can't your partner afford leisure clothes for you?"

She stiffened. "He doesn't buy my clothes."

"You'll never make me believe it," Jace replied coldly. "Those suits you wear didn't come out of anybody's bargain basement. The latest fashion, little girl, not castoffs, and you don't make that kind of money."

"Can't I make you understand that they're old?" she cried, exasperated. "I bought clothes with simple lines, Jace, so they wouldn't be dated!"

He flexed his shoulders as if the conversation had wearied him, and reached over to retrieve his shirt from the floor. "Nice try, Lady."

"I wish you wouldn't call me that," she said through her teeth. "Why can't you be like Duncan and just accept me the way I am without believing every horrible thing you can imagine about me?"

His eyes cut into hers. "Because I'm not Duncan. I never was." His jaw clenched. "Do you still want him? Is that why you came with Black?"

She threw up her hands. "All right. Yes, I want him. I'm after his money. I want to marry him and steal every penny he's got and buy ermine for all my friends! Now, are you satisfied?"

One dark eyebrow lifted nonchalantly. "I'll see you in

hell before I'll see you married to my brother," he said without heat.

Her eyes involuntarily lingered on his broad chest, the hard, unyielding set of his face that never softened, not even when he was in a gentler humor.

"Why do you hate me so?" she asked quietly.

His eyes darkened. "You damned well know why."

She dropped her gaze. "It was a long time ago," she reminded him. "And it isn't a pleasant memory."

"Why not?" he growled, his hand crumpling the shirt in his lap. "It would have solved your problems. You'd have been set for life, you and that flighty mother of yours."

"And all I'd have had to sacrifice was my self-respect," she murmured gently, glancing up at him. "I won't be any man's mistress, Jason, least of all yours."

He looked as if she'd slapped him, his eyes suddenly devoid of light. "Mistress?" he growled.

She lifted her chin proudly. "And what name would you have put on our relationship?" she challenged. "You asked me to live with you!"

"With me, that's right," he threw back. "In this house. My mother's house, damn you! Do you think her sense of propriety would have allowed anything less than a conventional relationship between us? I was proposing marriage, Amanda. I had the damned ring in my pocket if you'd stayed around long enough to see it."

Death must be like this, she thought, feeling a sting of pain so poignant it ran through her rigid body like a surge of electricity. Marriage! She could have been Jason Whitehall's wife, living with him, sharing everything with him...by now, she might have borne him a son...

Tears misted her eyes and, seeing them, a cruel, cold smile fleetingly touched his chiselled lips.

"Feeling regrets, honey?" he asked harshly. "I was on my way to the top about then. We were operating in the black for the first time, the first investments I'd made were just beginning to pay off. But you didn't stop to think about that, did you? You took one long look at me and slammed the door in my face. My God, you were lucky I didn't kick the door down and come after you."

"I expected you to," she admitted weakly, her eyes downcast, her heart breaking in half inside her rigid body. "I wouldn't even have blamed you. But you looked so fierce, Jason, and I was terrified of you physically. That's why I ran."

He stared at her. "Afraid of me? Why?"

She put the repackaged gauze back in the medicine cabinet. "You were very rough that night at my birthday party," she reminded him, blushing at the memory. "You can't imagine the secret terrors young girls have about men. Everything physical is so mysterious and unfamiliar. You were a great deal older than I was, and experienced, too. When you asked me so coolly to come and live with you, all I could think about was how it had been that night."

There was a long, blistering silence between them.

"I hurt you, didn't I?" he asked quietly, his eyes intent on her stiff back. "I meant to. Duncan told me that you only invited me out of courtesy, that you hated the sight of me." He laughed shortly. "He'd added a rider to the effect that you didn't think I'd know what to do with a woman."

She turned back toward him, the shock in her eyes. "I didn't tell him why I invited you," she said. Her head lowered. "The other part…I was teasing. Isn't it true that we sometimes joke about the things that frighten us most?"

she mused. "I was frightened of you, but I used to dream about how it would be if you kissed me." She turned away. "The dreams were...a little less harsh than the reality." She shrugged, laughing lightly to mask her pain. "It doesn't matter anymore. They were girlish dreams and I'm a woman now."

"Are you?" he asked, rising to tower over her in the small room, moving closer and smiling sarcastically at the quick backward step she took. "Twenty-three, and still afraid of me. I won't rape you, Amanda."

She flushed angrily. "Must you be so insulting?"

"I didn't think you could be insulted," he said coolly, his eyes stripping the clothes from her. "Poor little rich girl. What a comedown. How old is that thing you're wearing?"

"It covers me up," she said defensively.

"Barely," he replied. His eyes narrowed. "Mother mentioned something about buying you some clothes while you were here. Apparently she's seen more of your wardrobe than I have. But don't be tempted, honey," he added with a narrow glance. "I don't work like a fieldhand to keep you and that mother of yours in silks and satin. If you need clothes, you see to it that Black furnishes them, not Mother."

Her lower lip trembled. "I'd rather go naked than accept a white handkerchief that your money paid for," she said proudly.

"No doubt your boyfriend would prefer it, too," he said curtly.

"He's my partner!" she threw at him. "Nothing more."

"He's not much of a horseman, either," he added with a half-smile. "If he couldn't handle that tame mount Duncan put him on, how does he expect to handle you?"

She turned away. "What would you do for pleasure if I wasn't around to insult?" she asked wearily.

"Speaking of the devil, where is he?"

"Out by the pool with Duncan, discussing the account." She glanced at him icily. "Not that it's going to do any good. You'll just say no."

"Don't presume to think for me, Amanda," he said quietly. "You don't know me. You never have."

She licked her dry lips. "You don't let people get close to you, Jason."

"Would you like to?" he asked coolly.

"I don't think so, thanks," she murmured, turning. "You've had too many free shots at me already."

"Without justification?" he queried, moving closer. "My God, every time you come here there's another disaster."

"I didn't mean to hit the bull," she said defensively. "And you didn't have to yell...."

"What the hell did you expect me to do, get down on my knees and give thanks? You could have been killed, you crazy little fool," he growled.

"That would have suited you very well, wouldn't it?" she burst out. She turned away, just missing the expression on his face. "I meant to apologize, but I sprained my wrist and I couldn't even think for the pain."

"You sprained your wrist?" His eyes exploded. "And you drove from here to San Antonio like that? You damned little fool...!"

"What was I supposed to do, ask you for a ride?" she threw back, her brown eyes snapping at him. "You'd already shot the bull. I thought you might turn the gun on me if I didn't make myself scarce!"

She whirled and started out the door, ignoring his harsh tone as he called her name.

He caught up with her in the hall, catching her arm to swing her around, his eyes fierce under his jutting brow. With his shirt off, and that expanse of powerful bronzed muscles, he made her feel weak.

"Where do you think you're going?" he asked.

"To seduce Duncan by the pool," she said sweetly. "Isn't that why you think I came?"

"You'll never marry him." The threat was deliberate, calculated.

"I don't have to marry him to sleep with him, do I?" she asked with a toss of her long, silvery hair. "What's the matter, Jace, does it bother you that your brother might have succeeded where you failed?"

It was the wrong thing to say. She only got a second's warning before he started after her, but it was enough to make her turn and run. There was a peculiar elation in rousing Jace's temper. It made her feel alive, light-headed.

She ran into the living room and whirled to shut the door behind her, but she was too slow. Jace easily forced his way in, catching the door with his boot to slam it shut behind him, closing the two of them off from the world.

He stood facing her, his silver eyes blazing under his disheveled hair, his face hard and frankly dangerous, pagan-looking with his broad, bronzed chest bare, its pelt of dark hair glistening with sweat.

"Now let's see how brave you really are," he said in a voice deep and slow with banked anger as he began to move toward her.

She backed away from him slowly, all the courage

ebbing away at the look on his face. "I didn't mean it," she said breathlessly. "Jace, I didn't mean it!"

The desk caught her in the small of the back, halting her as effectively as a wall, and he closed the gap quickly, his hands catching her upper arms in a viselike grip that hurt.

"Don't," she pleaded, wincing. "You're hurting me!"

"You've been hurting me for years," he said in a rough undertone, his eyes blazing down into hers as he jerked her body against the hard, powerful length of his and pinned her to the desk in one smooth motion. "Has Duncan had you? Answer me!"

"No!" she whispered. "He's never touched me that way, never, Jace, I swear!"

She watched some of the strain leave his hard face even as she felt the tension grow in the powerful muscles of his legs where they pressed warmly into hers. His hands shifted around to her back. She wasn't wearing a bra under the terry-cloth dress, and she could feel his bare chest against her soft breasts through the thin fabric. The intimacy made her tremble.

He looked down at her, where her slender hands were pressed lightly against the mat of hair over his bronzed skin, and she was aware of the heavy, hard beat of his heart against the crushed warmth of her breasts.

"Is there anything but skin under this wisp of cloth?" he asked in a taut undertone. "I might as well be holding you in your underclothes."

"Jace!" she burst out, embarrassed.

"No, don't fight," he warned shortly when she tried to struggle away from him. His hands moved slowly, caressingly on her back, easing down below her waist to hold her tightly against the hard muscles of his thighs.

"Doesn't Black ever make love to you?" he asked curiously, watching the reaction in her flushed face, her frightened eyes. "You're too nervous for a woman who's used to being touched."

"Maybe I'm nervous because it's you," she burst out. Her fingers clenched together where they were forced to rest against his chest, as she fought not to give in to the longing to run her hands over his cool flesh. Her nostrils drank in the faint scent of cologne and leather that clung to his tall body.

"Because it's me?" he prompted, eyeing her.

She bit her lower lip nervously, all too aware of the privacy the closed door provided. "The last time, you hurt," she murmured.

"The last time you were sixteen years old and I was mad as hell," he reminded her. "I meant to hurt you."

"What did I do," she asked miserably, "except make the mistake of having a huge crush on you?"

He was so still, she thought for a moment that he hadn't heard her. His hands pressed into her soft flesh painfully for an instant, and a harsh sigh escaped from his lips.

"A crush on me?" he echoed blankly. "My God, you ran the other way every time I looked at you!"

"Of course I did—you terrified me!" she burst out, her eyes wide and dark and accusing as they met his. "I knew you and Mother didn't get along, and I thought you disliked me the way you did her. You were always and forever snapping at me or glaring."

His eyes ran over her face lightly, lingering pointedly on her mouth. "I suppose I was. I got the shock of my life when you invited me to that party."

She searched his hard face. "Why did you come?" she asked softly.

His shoulders rose and fell heavily. "I don't know," he admitted. "I was out of my element in more ways than one. I'd had women by then. I was used to females a hell of a lot more sophisticated than the crowd that surrounded me that night."

A surge of inexplicable jealousy ran riot through her body as she stared up at him. "So I gathered," she grumbled.

One dark eyebrow went up. "And how would you have known? You were obviously a virgin. I remember wondering at the time how many boys you'd kissed. You didn't even know enough to open your mouth to mine."

She lowered her eyes to his chest before he could see the embarrassed flush that spread down from her cheeks.

"I'd never been kissed by anyone," she said quietly. "You were…the first. You were almost the last, too," she added with an irrepressible burst of humor. "I was scared silly." Her eyes glanced up and down again. "It was a terribly adult kiss."

He lifted a lean hand and tilted her face up so that he could study it. "Did I leave scars on those young emotions?" he asked gently. "All I could remember about it later was the way you trembled against me, the softness of your body under my hands. I had a feeling I'd frightened you, but I was too angry to care. If I'd known the truth…"

"It probably wouldn't have made much difference," she put in. "I…get the feeling that you're not a gentle lover, Jason."

"Do you?" He drew her slowly up against him again, feeling the sudden tension in her body as his hands spread around her waist and trapped her there. "Maybe it's time I did something about that first impression."

"Jason, I don't think..." she began nervously.

"Shhhh," he whispered, bending his dark head. "We won't need words...it's been so long, Amanda," he murmured as his mouth brushed hers, his teeth nipping at her lower lip to make it part for him before his warm mouth moved on hers with a slow, lazy pressure that knocked any thought of resistance out of her mind. His arms swallowed her gently, folding her into his tall, powerful body while he taught her how much two people could tell each other with one long, slow kiss.

She could hardly believe it was happening, here in broad daylight, in the living room where they had sat like polite strangers the night before and never even touched.

It was almost like going back in time, to her sixteenth birthday party, but the kiss he'd given her then was nothing like this. He was easy with her, gentle, coaxing her mouth to open for him, to admit the deep, expert penetration of his tongue. The silence was only broken by the rough whisper of their breath as they kissed more and more hungrily. Her hands caressed his hair-roughened chest with an ardour that came not from experience, but from longing. She felt the need to touch, to explore, to learn the contours of his body with her fingers. She could feel the length of him, warm against her, and she trembled with the force of the new sensations he was arousing with the slow, caressing motions of his hands.

She felt his fingers move to the zipper at the front of the terry-cloth dress with a sense of wonder at his expertise. He was already beginning to slide it down when her nervous fingers caught at his and stilled them.

He drew back a breath, his eyes narrow and glittering with silver lights, his mouth sensuous, slightly swollen from the long, hard contact with hers.

"I want to look at you," he said huskily. "I want to watch your face when I touch you."

Shudders of wild sensation ran down her body like lightning. She realized with a start that she wanted his eyes on her, the touch of those hard fingers on her bare skin. But through the fog of hunger he'd created, she still remembered what the situation was between them. Jason was her enemy. He had nothing but contempt for her, and allowing him this kind of intimacy was suicide.

"No," she whispered tightly.

He lifted his face, looking down his arrogant nose at her. "Are we going to pretend that this is another first?" he asked curtly. "Sorry, honey, I'm an old fox now, and wary of woman-traps. I know one when I see one."

She tried to get away in a flurry of anger, but he held her effortlessly. "Let go of me!" she cried. "I don't know what you're talking about!"

"No?" he returned coldly. "You're full of tricks all right, Amanda, but don't think you'll catch me. Deliberate provocation can be dangerous, and you'd better think twice before you try it again. Next time, I'll take you," he said harshly, watching the shock darken her eyes, "and teach you things about men you never knew."

"I wouldn't let you!" she burst out.

"Why not?" His eyes were faintly insulting as he released her abruptly. "Women like you aren't all that particular, are they? Why not me, Amanda?"

"I hate you!" she whispered unsteadily, and at the moment, she meant it. How dare he make insinuations about her?

He only smiled, but there was no humor in his look. "Do you? I'm glad, Amanda, I'd hate to think you were dying of unrequited love for me. But if you change your mind, honey, you know where my room is," he added for good measure. "Just don't expect marriage. I know how badly you and your mother need a meal ticket. But, honey," he said, as he opened the door, "it won't be me."

He went out, closing the door behind him.

Chapter Five

She went to her room to freshen up, and bathed her hot cheeks in cold water. She held a cold cloth to her lips as well, hoping that might make the bruised swelling go down. Bruised. Her eyes closed, her heart turned over, in memory. Her mind went back to the day Jace had approached her with his earth-shattering proposition.

It had been a day much like this one, sunny and warm, and Amanda had been alone when she'd heard a car drive up in front of the house. She'd gone onto the porch as Jace took the steps three at a time. He was dressed in denims, and had obviously been out working with his hands on the ranch. He'd stopped just in front of her, oddly irritated, sweeping the black Stetson off his dark head. His silver eyes had glittered down at her out of a deeply tanned face.

"You look like death on a holiday," he commented gruffly, tracing the unusually thin lines of her slender body with eyes that lingered. "How's it going?"

She'd drawn herself erect, too proud to let him see what a burden it all was—her father's death, Bea's careless spending, the loss of their assets, the disgrace—and met his eyes bravely.

"We're coping," she'd said. She even forced a cool smile for him.

But Jace, being Jace, hadn't bought it. Those narrow, piercing eyes had seen through her pose easily. He was a businessman, accustomed to coping with minds shrewder and more calculating than Amanda's, and with the knowledge of long acquaintance, he could read her as easily as a newspaper.

"I hear you've had to put the house itself on the market," he said frankly. "At the rate your mother's going, before long you'll be selling the clothes off your back to support her."

Her lower lip had threatened to give her away even more, but she'd caught it in her teeth just in time. "I'll manage."

"You don't have to manage, Amanda," he said curtly. There was a curious hesitation in him, a stillness that should have warned her. But it hadn't. "I can make it right for you. Pay the bills, keep the ranch going. I can even support that scatterbrained parent of yours, though the thought disgusts me."

She'd eyed him warily. "In exchange for what, exactly?" she'd asked.

"Come and live with me," he said.

The words had hit her like ice water. Unexpected, faintly embarrassing, their impact had left her white. She was afraid of Jason; terrified of him on any physical level. Perhaps if he'd been gentler that night when he'd surprised her by showing up for her birthday party...but he hadn't, and the thought of what he was asking turned her blood cold. She hadn't even bothered to explain. She'd turned around before he had time to react, rushed into the house, slammed and locked the door behind her, all without a word. And the memory of that day had been between them ever since, like a thorny fence neither cared to climb.

It was a blessing that Jace thought her instinctive response to him was an act. If he'd known the truth, that she quite simply couldn't resist him in any way, it would have been unbearable for her. Jace would love having a weapon like that to use on her. And if he knew what she really felt...it didn't bear consideration.

Love. There was no way that she could deny the feeling. What a tragedy that all her defenses had finally deserted her, and bound her over to the enemy. This gossamer, sweet kind of sensation made her want to laugh and sing and cry all at once, to run to Jace with her arms outstretched and offer him anything, everything, to share her life with him, to give him sons....

Tears misted her eyes. Tess would give him those. Perfect sons with perfect minds, always neat, very orderly, made to stand around like little statues. Tess would see to that, and Jace was too busy to bother. He wanted heirs, not love. It wasn't a word he knew.

Why did it have to be Jace? she asked in anguish. Why not Terry, or Duncan, or the half dozen other men she'd dated over the years? Why did it have to be the one man in the world she couldn't have. Her poor heart would wear itself out on Jace's indifference.

It was a good thing that she and Terry were leaving at

the end of the week. Now that she knew what her fear of Jace really was, she could stay away from him. She could leave Casa Verde and never see him again. The tears came back, hot and bitter. How terribly that hurt, to think of never seeing him again. But in the long run, it would be less cruel than tormenting herself by being near him.

Resolutely, she dried the tears and exchanged the aqua lounging dress for her jeans and a pink top. She crumpled the dress into her suitcase, vowing silently that she'd never wear it again. As she tucked it away, she caught the faint scent of the tangy cologne Jace wore, clinging to the fabric.

Marguerite was busily addressing dainty decal-edge envelopes in her sitting room on the second floor when Amanda joined her.

"Hello, dear, have enough sun?" the older woman asked pleasantly, pausing with her pen in midair.

"In a sense," she replied. "I came in to lend you a hand but then I ran into Jace and stopped to patch him up."

Marguerite's face changed, drew in. "Is he all right?"

"Yes, it was just a gash in his arm," she replied, easing the fears she could read plainly in the older woman's eyes. "I never did find out how it happened. One of the cows, I guess."

Marguerite's dark eyes hardened. "Those horrible beasts," she exclaimed. "Sometimes I think the Whitehall men have more compassion for breeding stock than they do for women! Except for Duncan, bless him."

Amen, Amanda thought as she pulled over a dainty wing chair next to Marguerite's writing table and sat down.

"Jace actually let you put a bandage on him?" she asked

her young companion. "I'd have thought little Tess would have been standing by just in case."

"Apparently not," she replied, hoping her face didn't show any of what really happened. What she didn't know was that her mouth was still swollen, despite the cold compress, and there were marks on one delicate cheek, which were plainly made by the rasp of a man's slightly burred cheek.

But Marguerite kept her silence, aware of the peculiar tension in her companion. "You're sure you don't mind helping?" she asked, pushing some envelopes and a page of names and addresses toward her.

"Of course not." Amanda took a pen and began to write in her lovely longhand.

"Jace didn't argue about letting you play nurse?" she continued gently.

"He did at first," she murmured.

Marguerite glanced at her, amused. "You're coming to the party, of course," she said. "These are just unforgivably late invitations to a few friends whom I'm sure can make it despite the short notice. The party's going to be held at the Sullevans'. They have a huge ballroom, something we haven't."

Amanda nodded, remembering the enormous Sullevan estate with its graceful curves and gracious hospitality. "I can't come, you know," she said gently.

Marguerite looked across at her with a knowing smile. "I'll get you a dress."

"No!" Amanda burst out, horrified as she remembered Jace's threat.

But Marguerite's attention was already back on the invitations. Amanda started to write, unaware of the faint, amused smile on the older woman's face.

* * *

Duncan and Marguerite were the only ones at the breakfast table when Amanda went downstairs after a restless night. Jace, she was told, had long since gone to his office, in a black temper.

"He gets worse every day lately," Duncan remarked, glancing at Amanda with a smile as she took the seat beside him. "You wouldn't know why, Amanda?"

She tried to hide her red face by bending it over her cup of black coffee. "Me? Why?"

"Well, you were both conspicuously absent from the supper table," he observed. "You had a sick headache, and Jace had some urgent business at the office."

Marguerite was just beginning to make connections. One silver eyebrow went up in a gesture reminiscent of her eldest son. "Did you and Jace argue yesterday, Amanda?" she asked gently.

"It's downright dangerous to have them in the same room together lately," Duncan teased. "He flies at her and she flies right back. God help anyone who gets between them."

"Where's Terry, I wonder?" Amanda hedged, helping herself to some scrambled eggs and little fat sausages.

"He and I were up late discussing the campaign," Duncan explained. "He's probably overslept. I've got to fly to New York today on business." He sipped his coffee, set the china cup down gently in its saucer, and stared at Amanda. "Jace agreed to talk with Terry tonight."

"Did he? That's nice," she murmured.

He studied her downbent head, reading accurately the wan, drawn look about her face, the dark circles under her eyes.

Marguerite finished her breakfast and crumpled her

napkin beside her plate, lifting her coffee cup with a smile. "How lovely to have one uninterrupted meal." She sighed. "Duncan, breakfast with you is so restful."

"I don't own controlling interest in the properties," he reminded her.

The words reminded Amanda of what Jace had said, and she winced unconsciously.

Marguerite's dark eyes flashed. "I'd like to get rid of it all," she grumbled, "except for a little of the ranch. Maybe we weren't so wealthy in the old days, but at least we could eat a meal without someone being called away on business. And Jace didn't push himself so hard."

"Didn't he?" Duncan asked gently. "He always has. And we both know why."

Marguerite smiled at him wistfully. "And what do you think about the result?"

"I think there's a distinct possibility of success," he said mysteriously, lifting his coffee cup as if in a toast.

"You people do carry on the strangest conversations," Amanda remarked between mouthfuls.

"Sorry, dear," Marguerite apologized nicely. "Just old suspicions."

"Want to come to New York with me?" Duncan asked Amanda suddenly. "I'm just going for the day. We'll ride the ferry over to Staten Island and make nasty remarks about the traffic."

Her eyes lit up. The prospect of being carefree for one whole day was enchanting, especially when she wanted so desperately to keep out of Jace's way.

"Could I?" she asked, and her whole face changed, grew younger. "Oh, but Terry..." she murmured, her enthusiasm dampening.

"He'll be just fine with me," Marguerite said cheerfully. "I'll take care of him for you, and tonight he and Jace will be busy discussing the accounts. So why not go, dear? You look as if you could use a little gaiety."

"If you don't mind..."

"Go put on a pretty dress," Duncan told her, grinning. "I'll give you a whole half hour."

"Done!" Amanda said excitedly. She excused herself from the table and darted upstairs. It was like being a child again. She'd forgotten the magic of being wealthy enough to take off and go anywhere, anytime. The Whitehalls took it for granted just as Amanda had once, but those days were long past. Now she had to budget everything, especially groceries. Trips and holidays were something she could no longer afford.

She changed into a white sundress with yellow daisies on the bodice and a full eyelet skirt, a delightful little frock she'd found on sale at a small boutique last fall. She scooped up her lightweight tan sweater and slipped on her sandals in a rush, barely stopping long enough to check her makeup and add another pin to the hair she had carefully tucked into a neat chignon. She forgot her purse and had to go back for it. Not that there was more than a few dollars in it, but she felt more secure having it.

She darted downstairs to find that Terry had finally made it to the breakfast table. He looked sleepy and faintly hung over, but he grinned at Amanda pleasantly.

"Hi!" she said. "I'm doing to desert you and go to New York, okay?"

"Sure. Have a good time. I'll work on my sales pitch out by the pool," he told her.

"Just don't fall in. He can't swim," she told the others with a laugh.

"We can't all be fish like you in the water," came the teasing reply.

"If you're ready," Duncan said, slipping into his brown suit coat.

"More than," Amanda told him.

He studied her outfit carefully, and his eyes narrowed on the sweater. "Honey, there's a lot of difference between Texas and New York, and we'll be leaving after dark. Are you sure that sweater's going to be enough on your arms?"

Amanda nodded, too proud to admit that the only coat she owned was back in San Antonio, and that it wouldn't have done for anything more than a trip to the neighborhood grocery.

"I'll loan you my spring coat," Marguerite said easily, smiling. "You simply can't pack coats, Duncan, they're too bulky," she added.

Amanda blessed her for that, knowing the older woman had deliberately covered up for her.

Marguerite came back with a lightweight gray coat, very stylish, and very expensive.

"But I can't..." Amanda protested.

"Of course you can, dear. I have several more, and we're about the same size. Here, try it on."

She helped Amanda into it, and it was a perfect fit. Her soft brown eyes said it all, and Marguerite only nodded.

"Have fun, now, and don't be too late. Which plane are you taking?"

"The Cessna," Duncan called back as they went out the front door. "Don't keep supper for us—we'll have it there."

The twin-engine plane made good time, and Duncan

was a good pilot. Almost as good as Jace, and not quite as daring. Before Amanda knew it, they were landing in New York's sprawling terminal, despite the wait to be sandwiched in between jumbo jets.

Duncan hailed them a taxi with the flair of an experienced traveler and hustled Amanda inside. He gave the driver an address and leaned back with a sigh.

"Now, this is the way to travel," he told her. "No bags, no toothbrush, just leap on a plane and go."

She laughed, catching his exuberant mood. "Sure. Since we've come this far, let's just go on to Martinique."

"Now, there was a fun island," he replied, going back in time. "Remember when you and I flew down there with Uncle Macklin and forgot to tell Mother? I thought the end of the world was coming when they caught up with us. But we had fun, didn't we?"

"We certainly did," she replied, turning her head against the seat to look at him. He was nothing like Jace. She liked his boyish face, his sparkling personality. If only she could have loved him.

"I hate it when you do that," he remarked, grinning.

"Do what?" she asked softly.

"Measure me against Jace. Oh, don't both to deny it," he said when she started to protest. "I've known you too long. Anyway, I don't really mind. Jace is one of a kind. Most men would fall short of him by comparison."

She let her eyes drift to the moving meter. "Sorry. I wasn't trying to be mean."

His hand found hers and squeezed it. "I know that. The joy of being with you, Mandy, is that I can be myself. I'm glad to have you for a friend."

She smiled at him. "Same here."

"Of course, it wasn't always friendship," he said, lifting a corner of his mouth. "I had a crush on you when you were about sixteen. You didn't even notice—you were too busy trying to keep out of Jace's way. I was terribly jealous, you know."

"Did you, really?" she asked. "Duncan, I'm so sorry…!" Maybe that explained the lie he'd told Jace about her reason for inviting him to the long-ago birthday party.

"Just a crush, darling, and I got over it fast. I'm glad I did. It was never there for you, was it?" he asked, more serious than she'd ever seen him.

"No," she said honestly. "It never was."

"If I can help, Mandy, in any way, I will," he said suddenly.

His kindness, coming on the heels of Jace's antagonism, was her undoing. Hot tears swelled up in her eyes and overflowed onto her cheeks in a silent flood.

"Mandy," he said sympathetically, and drew her gently against him, rocking her softly while she cried. "Poor little mite, it's been rough, hasn't it? I should have been keeping in touch. You need looking after."

She shook her head. "I can take care of myself," she mumbled.

"Sure you can, darling." He laughed gently, patting her shoulder.

"It's just…if I could will Mama to somebody with tremendous assets," she laughed.

"Some rich man will come along and save you eventually," he told her. "After all, your mama is still a beautiful woman. Sweet, intelligent…"

"…addlepated and selfish," she finished with a wry grin, drawing back to pull a handkerchief from her purse and dab at her wet eyes with it. “I don’t usually give in to self-pity. Sorry. It gets to be a heavy load sometimes, having all the responsibility.”

“Which you shouldn’t, at your age,” he said tautly. “You haven’t been able to do anything but support her since it all happened. I know you don’t mind, but the fact is, you’re not being allowed a life of your own. All you’re doing is working to keep Bea up. There’s nothing left for you to enjoy after you pay the bills, and it isn’t fair, Amanda.”

“Duncan, if I don’t do it, who will?” she asked gently. “Mother can’t work. She’s never had to. What would she do?”

“People could rent her, an hour at a time, to stand in the corner and look beautiful while holding a lamp or something,” he suggested.

She burst out laughing at the idea. “You’re horrible.”

“That’s why you like me,” he returned. “Amanda, remember the summer we tied bows on Jace’s sale bulls just before that auction?”

She whistled softly. “Do I ever! We’d never have outrun him if you hadn’t got that brilliant idea to turn out all his brood mares as we went through the barn.”

“That made him even madder,” he recalled. “I went to spend a week with my aunt that very evening, before Jace got back from the sale. And you, if I remember rightly, went away immediately to boarding school.”

“I felt it would be safer living in Switzerland at that point in my life.” She grinned. “He was furious!”

He sighed. “They were good days, weren’t they, Amanda?”

She nodded. “What a shame that we have to grow up and become dignified.”

Chapter Six

They were homeward bound when some unfamiliar sound woke her. She sat straight up in the seat to find Duncan struggling with the controls, his face more somber than she'd seen it in years.

"What's the matter?" she asked with a worried frown.

He was bending slightly forward, one hand on the wheel, the other on the instrument panel. "I think it's the left mag, but I can't tell yet."

"Mag?" she echoed.

"Magneto." He reached for the ignition switch and turned it momentarily left and then right. The plane was literally doing a hula in midair. Duncan gritted his teeth. "I'm going to try different power settings and ease in on the mixture, then I'll know if we can risk going on," he mumbled to himself.

She just stared, the language he was speaking vaguely

incomprehensible to her. But whatever he was doing, it didn't seem to help. The vibration in the plane was terrible.

He cursed under his breath. "Well, that's it. We'll have to put it down at Seven Bridges and have it fixed. I won't risk going any farther like this."

Duncan nosed the Cessna down where the string of runway lights stretched like a double strand of glowing pearls through a low-lying mist.

"God, I hope there's not a cow on the landing strip," he mumbled as he held the vibrating airplane on course.

"You're such a comfort to me, Duncan," she said, biting back her nervousness. "Where did you say we were?"

"Seven Bridges, Tennessee." He grinned. "Hang on, honey, here goes."

"I trust you," she told him. "We'll be okay."

"I sure as hell hope so."

The next few minutes were the most dangerous Amanda could ever remember. The engines felt as if they were trying to shake apart, and the landing lights in that fog were a little blurry. If Jace had been at the controls, she'd never have worried at all...she was sorry she had to think of that, knowing that Duncan was doing his best. But Jace had steel nerves, and his younger brother, despite his flight experience in the twin-engine plane, didn't. Once, as he put the plane down, he lost control for just a split second and had to pull up and come around again, an experience that threatened to turn Amanda's hair white.

Her hands gripped the edge of her seat so hard that she could feel the leather give under them, but not a word passed her lips. Nothing she said would help, and it might distract Duncan fatally. She kept quiet and whispered a prayer.

Duncan eased the plane down, his eyes on the controls, the landing strip, the airspeed indicator, the artificial horizon, the altimeter. Now training was taking over, he relaxed visibly, and put the twin-engine plane carefully down the runway with a gentle screeching noise followed by a downgrading of the engine, and sudden, total silence as he cut the power entirely and taxied in.

"In the veritable nick of time." He sighed wearily.

"You done good, as they say," she teased, able to relax now that they were safe. "Now, how do we get home?"

"Hitchhike?" he suggested with a grin.

"Call for reinforcements?" she suggested.

"Reinforcements would be Jace," he reminded her, "and my jaw hasn't healed from the last time I upset him."

She hadn't thought about that. They'd promised to be home by midnight, and it was…she sighed deeply.

"Shall we see if the gentleman has a house for rent with a good view," she asked with a nervous laugh, "and maybe a couple of jobs open?"

"At this point, it might be wise to consider the folly of going home."

They climbed out of the plane in the rear and the fixed base operator approached them out of a lighted hangar wiping his hands on a rag. He was a big, aging man with a shock of white hair and a toothy smile.

"Thought I heard a plane," he grinned. "Got problems?"

"One of my magnetos went out on me," Duncan told him. "I'm going to need a new one. If you've got one you can put on for me."

"What is she? A Cessna by the look," he guessed, and Duncan nodded. "Sure, I can fix it, I think. I run an aviation service, and the wife and I live in that trailer over there." He chuckled. "I couldn't sleep, so I came down here to wrestle with a rewiring job in an old Aeronca Champion I just bought. Well, let's have a look at your problem."

Minutes later, Amanda was comfortably seated in Donald Aiken's trailer with his small, dark-haired wife, Annette, enjoying the best cup of coffee she'd ever tasted while she recuperated from the hair-raising experience.

They were discussing the economy when Duncan and the airport operator walked in.

"Donald can fix it," Duncan said with a tired grin. He needed a shave, and looked it, but at this hour of the morning it didn't really matter.

"Thank goodness." She sighed. "You know, we really do need to call your mother. We can make her promise not to tell Jace…."

"Uh, I'm afraid you won't be calling anybody long-distance," Donald said apologetically. "Or locally either for the time being. Cable got cut, and they're still trying to fix it. I heard over the radio earlier while I was working. And you can't get a decent cell phone signal anywhere around here. Sure am sorry."

Duncan sighed. "It's fate," he said, nodding. "Out to get me."

"I'll protect you, Duncan," Amanda promised.

"Unless I miss my guess, you're going to need protection as much as I am." He shook his head. "Well, can't be helped."

"It won't take long," Donald said encouragingly, finishing a quick cup of coffee. "We'll have you on your way in no time," he promised.

No time turned out to be two hours, and it was thanks

to Donald's skill as a mechanic that they were able to take off at all.

The sun had not yet risen when Duncan set the twin-engine plane down on the Casa Verde landing strip, but the sky was already lightening with the approaching dawn.

Tired and bedraggled, they got out of the plane and stood quietly on the apron looking around at the quiet, pastoral landscape.

"Peaceful, isn't it?" Duncan asked, taking a deep breath of fresh air.

"So far," she agreed with a wan smile. "They'll have heard us land, of course."

"It's never failed yet."

As if in answer to the remark, they heard the loud, angry roar of one of the ranch's pickup trucks.

"Would you care to bet who's driving it?" Duncan asked with cool nonchalance.

"Oh, I think I have some idea," she returned. Her knees felt curiously weak. Circumstance it might have been, but she knew without guessing what Jace's reaction was going to be, and she wanted to run. But there was no place to go. Jace was already out of the truck and striding toward them with homicide in his eyes.

He hadn't slept. That registered in Amanda's tired mind even as his dangerous gaze riveted itself to Duncan as he approached them. He needed a shave badly, and his face was pale and haggard. He was wearing gray suit pants with a half unbuttoned white shirt, and over it was his suede ranch coat. The familiar black Stetson was pulled cockily over one eye, and he looked fierce and uncivilized in the gray half-light.

"Uh, hi, Jace," Duncan said uneasily.

He'd barely got the words out when Jace reached him, hauling back to throw a deadly accurate right fist into his jaw and knock him sprawling backward onto the pavement.

"Do you know what we've been through?" Jace breathed huskily, his temper barely leashed. "We expected you by midnight and it's daylight. You let us sit here without even a phone call… Mother's in tears, damn you!"

"It's a long story," Duncan muttered, holding his jaw as he sat up, his face contrite. "I swear to God, we've had a night ourselves. The right magneto went in one of the engines and I almost crashed the plane getting us down."

She could have sworn Jace paled. His glittering eyes shot to Amanda and ran over her like hands feeling for breaks after a fall. "Are you all right?" he asked curtly.

She nodded, afraid to risk words. She'd never seen him like this.

Duncan picked himself up, feeling his jaw gingerly. "Damn, Jace, I wish you'd yell instead of hit," he mused, geared to his brother's temper after years of conditioning.

"What happened?" came the terse reply.

Duncan explained briefly the events that had mounted up to delay them, adding that they couldn't even telephone.

Jace's face got, if possible, even harder. "You could still have phoned before you left New York," he reminded his brother.

Duncan smiled sheepishly. "I know. But we were having such a good time that I just didn't think. Then, when we finally got to the airport, I was afraid to waste the time."

"I even tried to call the terminal in New York to find out when you filed your flight plan," Jace continued grimly.

"Guilty on all counts," Duncan agreed. "I don't have a good excuse. I just...didn't think."

Jace's bloodshot eyes narrowed. "I'm going to let you explain that to Mother."

Duncan waited for Amanda, who'd been quiet, and held out his hand, but Jace got to her first, catching her arm in a grip that was frankly punishing. His eyes went over the expensive coat and narrowed.

"You didn't have a coat with you," he said, his tone challenging.

"No..." she started to explain.

"Didn't I warn you about gifts?" he demanded.

It was too much. The night, the near-crash, the worry about getting home and then Jace's fury...it was just too much. A sob broke from her throat and she started crying, little noises escaping her tight throat, tears rolling pathetically down her cheeks.

"Oh, for God's sake, Amanda...!" Jace burst out.

"Leave her alone, Jace," Duncan said quietly, and stopped to draw her against him. "I scared her out of her wits. And if the coat bothers you, blame Mother. Amanda didn't have one and Mother loaned it to her."

Jace looked as if he wanted to throw things. But he whirled without another word, his face terrible, and got in behind the wheel of the truck. Duncan eased Amanda into the seat first, watching her shrink away from contact with Jace when he got in on the other side of her and closed the door. Jace started the truck and left rubber behind taking off.

They had to go over the explanations again for Marguerite, who was pale and worn out from crying, hugging the two of them as if they'd come back from the dead. To

Amanda's silent relief, Jace disappeared upstairs as soon as they got home. She couldn't cope with him right now.

"I'm so glad you're safe." Marguerite sniffed, sipping black coffee with a sodden handkerchief clutched in one thin hand. "I was so worried."

"I wish we could have let you know," Amanda said gently, wiping her own face, "but there wasn't any way. I'm so sorry we upset you."

"Jace more than me," she said with a damp smile. "He wore ruts in my carpet. I've never seen him so upset."

"He hit Duncan," Amanda said, faintly resentful.

"Duncan deserved it," the injured party said sheepishly, "and you know it."

Marguerite sighed. "You're lucky that's all he did. He threatened worse things while we waited."

"Would anyone mind if I went to bed for what's left of the night?" Amanda asked gently. "I know you two are just as tired as I am, but…"

"You go right ahead, dear," Marguerite said with an affectionate smile. "Duncan and I will be right behind you. Rest well."

"Where's Terry, by the way?" Amanda asked suddenly, remembering him belatedly.

"He went to bed early and we didn't wake him," Marguerite explained. "He's missed all the excitement."

Amanda smiled wanly. "I'll see you both later, and I really am sorry," she added gently, bending to kiss Marguerite's cheek as she passed her.

The fatigue and lack of sleep hit her all at once when she got to her room. She took off the sundress and her sandals, but she couldn't seem to stay awake long enough to get out of her slip and hose before she drifted off in a heap at the foot of the bed.

Through a fog, she felt herself being lifted and placed under something soft and cool. Her heavy eyelids opened slowly, as if in a dream, to find a hard, tanned face looming over her.

"Sleepy?" he asked in a voice too soft to be Jace's.

She nodded. Her vision was blurred, as if she was dreaming. Perhaps she was.

He brought the cover up to her waist, his eyes lingering on the lacy bodice of her slip where it exposed the soft, pale swell of her breasts.

"I'm not dressed," she murmured drowsily.

"I can see that," he replied softly, with an amused smile.

"You're mad at me," she recalled, frowning. "I don't remember…why…but…"

"Don't think. Go to sleep."

Her eyes drifted down to the growth of beard on his tanned face and involuntarily her fingers reached up to touch it. For a dream, he felt warmly real.

"You haven't slept either," she whispered.

"I couldn't, until I knew," he said gruffly.

"Were you really worried?" she asked.

"Worried!" He laughed shortly, but his eyes were still turbulent with emotion. "My God, I had visions of the two of you lying mangled in the wreckage of the Cessna. And you were going up and down Broadway!"

She dropped her eyes to his broad chest where his shirt was unbuttoned, and the curling dark hairs on the bronzed skin were damp, like the hair on his head, as if he'd just come from a shower.

"We were having fun," she said inadequately.

"You always had fun with him." There was a world of bitterness in the words.

"And I always ran from you," she murmured gently. Her fingers traced the long, chiseled curve of his warm mouth. "I could never get close to you," she told him, weariness making her vulnerable, loosening her tongue. "The day I invited you to the party, I was scared to death. I wanted you to come so much, and you were like stone."

"Self-defense, Amanda," he replied quietly, his eyes slow and bold on the lacy white slip and the white flesh peeking out of it. "I didn't like the way you made me feel. I didn't like being vulnerable either."

She laughed wistfully. "All I ever managed to do was make you lose your temper."

"Are you sure?" He caught her hand and drew it to his warm, hard chest, pressing its palm against the hard, shuddering beat of his heart. "Feel what you do to me," he murmured, watching the surprise in her sleepy eyes. "I can look at you and my heart damned near beats me to death. It's been that way for years and you've never even noticed."

Her lips fell open, in astonishment. Jace had always been so self-sufficient, so controlled. It was new and exciting to consider the possibility that she could do this to him, that she could make him feel the same shuddering excitement that filled her when he touched her.

"I think...I was afraid to notice," she whispered shakily, "because I wanted it so much...."

His breath was coming hard and fast now, his eyes going down to her softly parted lips. Like a man in a trance, he bent his head, his eyes staring straight into hers.

The tension between them was almost unbearable. She

could feel the warm, smoky sigh of his breath on her lips, the slight mingling scents of soap and cologne as he bent over her, the blazing warmth of his body where her cool hands were pressed against his chest.

"Jason..." she whispered apprehensively.

His open mouth brushed against her lips while he watched her. "Hush," he whispered gently. "I only want to touch you, to taste you, to be sure that you're here and safe and not lying in a field somewhere torn to pieces. God, I've never been so afraid!"

"You shouted at me," she reminded him, the words muffled against his mouth as it brushed and caressed in a maddening, tantalizing motion.

"You'd scared me out of my wits. What did you expect?" he growled. He moved, leaning both arms on the sheet on either side of her, his chest arching over hers as he studied her flushed face. "You little fool, can't you get it into your head that I'm not rational when it comes to you? Does it give you some kind of juvenile kick to knock me off-balance, the way you did in the living room?"

She studied his hard mouth quietly, loving the chiseled perfection of it, the sensations it could cause. "I never realized before that I *could*...knock you off-balance."

His eyes dropped to the brief, almost transparent bodice of her slip. "Lying there so soft and sweet," he murmured, "and I'm making small talk when all I want out of life right now is to strip you down to your skin and taste every silky inch of you."

Her heart turned over. "What time is it?" she asked quickly.

"You're afraid, aren't you?" He lifted his hand and touched, very lightly, the soft swell of her breast with his hard fingers, smiling when she caught them and moved them to her shoulder. "You did that once before," he reminded her. "At that party, years ago. I carried the memory around like a faded photograph for years. You were so deliciously innocent." His eyes darkened, his face tautened. "And now you're a woman, not so innocent, so why pretend?"

She chewed on her lower lip, too weary to deny it, to fight with him. "I'm tired, Jason," she whispered meekly.

He took a deep breath. "And I'm not?" he asked. His eyes searched hers. "I've been pacing up and down in my room, trying to get myself back together. I know that if I try to get some sleep, every time I shut my eyes I'll see the look on your face when I jumped on you about the damned coat."

"But Marguerite…" she began.

"Insisted. I know, Duncan told me, remember?" He smoothed the hair away from her face. "I was worried sick, honey," he said quietly. "And hurt."

"I couldn't hurt you," she whispered curiously.

"Couldn't you?" His eyes dropped to her mouth. "You don't know how much you could hurt me," he murmured, bending. He eased her mouth under his, cherishing it, touching it lightly, gentling it in a silence that was only broken by the sound of a breeze outside the open window and the soft sigh of Jace's breath while he kissed her.

She reached up to hold him, but he caught her hands and spread them against his cool, broad chest, tangling her fingers in the mat of curling dark hair.

"Have you ever learned how to touch a man?" he asked against her parted lips.

She caressed him with nervous, unsure hands while the touch of his tormenting mouth drove her slowly mad.

"Kiss me hard," she whispered achingly, her slitted eyes looking up into his.

"In a minute." A faint triumphant smile touched his mouth. "I like it like this, don't you? Slow and easy. I like to hold back as long as I can—it makes everything more intense," he whispered against her lips. "Come on, honey, don't just lie there and let me do it all. Help me."

She almost blurted out that she didn't know how, that her only intimate experience had been with him. With other men she had never gone beyond kissing.

She opened her mouth to his and reached up to hold him, to draw his heavy, warm body against hers so that he was half-lying across her, the crushing pressure of his weight dragging a moan from her throat.

"Not so hard, baby," he whispered, drawing back a little to look at her. "It's been a long time since I made any effort to go slow with a woman. Let it be gentle with us, this time."

The words awed her, touched her. She reached up and traced his hard mouth with her fingertip, her dark eyes searching his light ones while her heart hammered in her throat. "I don't know much..." she blurted out, the admission not quite what she meant it to be.

"It's all right," he said quietly. He smoothed her lips under his softly, slowly. "Don't you want to touch me?" he whispered, and his fingers drew against her waist, her rib cage, up to the soft, high curve of her breasts. "God knows, I want to touch you," he added huskily, and his hands moved to cup her soft breasts with a light touch that made her tremble all the same and catch at his fingers wildy.

He drew back, studying the apprehension in her eyes watchfully. "I won't hurt you," he said softly.

"I know. I…" She stared up at him helplessly. "I need time," she whispered.

He drew in a hard, heavy breath, leaning his weight on his forearms as he poised just above her. "You've had seven years," he reminded her.

"You've hated me for seven years," she corrected sadly. "Jason, you can't expect me to…to trust you…to give…"

He reached down and kissed her roughly. "To give yourself to me—why can't you say it?" His eyes narrowed. "All right, I'll accept that. You need time to get used to the idea, and I'll give you that. But not much, Amanda. I've waited longer than I ever intended already, and I'm damned near the end of my rope. I've gone a hell of a long time without a woman."

She gasped at him and would have pursued that, but he bent suddenly and she felt the firm, warm pressure of his mouth against the bare curve of her breast where the strap had fallen away. Her body arched instinctively at the unexpected pressure, at the newness of a man's lips on her body, and she gasped.

"Do you like it?" he murmured against her silky skin, and drew the strap down even farther to seek the deep pink peak with his warm mouth in an intimacy that made her grasp his dark hair with both hands to jerk him away. A mistake, she saw that immediately, because his eyes had a brief and total view of the curves his lips had touched, before she was able to jerk the bodice back in place.

He studied her flaming face with interest. "Was it always in the dark before?" he murmured, smiling. "I'm glad you left at least one first for me. What's that saying about the delights to be found in small packages?"

"You beast!" she whispered, flushing more wildly than ever.

He chuckled softly, watching her jerk the sheet over herself. He sat up, as smug as a tiger with one paw on its prey.

"Small but perfect, love," he said gently, and for a moment he seemed a stranger, his silver eyes almost gentle, his face faintly kind.

Impulsively, she reached out and touched his bare chest, looking up at him with all the unasked questions in her eyes. "I'm sorry you and Marguerite were worried."

He only nodded. "You'd better get some sleep."

"You had, too," she murmured. "You won't be able to work at all."

"I'll have hell keeping my mind on work, all right," he admitted, staring into her puzzled eyes. He leaned down, his mouth poised just over hers. "Hard, this time," he whispered gruffly, "and open your mouth...."

He crushed her lips under his, fostering a hunger like nothing she'd ever felt before. It was a meeting of mouths that was as intimate as the merging of two souls. She arched up against him, her mouth wild, her nails biting into his shoulders, moaning in a surrender as sweeping as death. She loved him so, wanted him so, and for this instant he was hers. She wanted nothing more than to give him everything she had to give, despite all the arguments, all the harsh words.

He drew back, breathing heavily, his eyes blazing with suppressed desire. He caught her wrists and drew her hands gently away from his shoulders, easing her back down on the pillow.

"I'd rather saw off my arm than leave you," he said in a husky whisper. "Oh, God, I want you so!"

She caught her trembling lower lip in her teeth, staring up at him helplessly, beyond words.

He drew a heavy breath and leaned down, brushing her mouth lightly with his, a tender caress after the storm. "You could still sleep with me," he remarked quietly, searching her misty eyes. "No strings, just sleep. I'd like to hold you against me, see you lying there in my bed."

The flush went all the way down her body, and he watched it with a passing confusion in his glittering eyes.

"What if your mother or Duncan happened to walk in?" she asked unsteadily, trying to make light of it when she wanted nothing more than to do just as he'd suggested.

He searched her eyes. "Then I'd have to marry you, wouldn't I?" he asked with a faint smile. He got up before she could decide whether or not he was joking, and the moment was lost. He glanced back at her from the open door.

"Sweet dreams, honey. Sleep well. God knows, I won't," he added, his eyes sweeping the length of her body under the thin sheet.

"Good night, Jason," she whispered softly, "or should I say good morning?"

He smiled, then turned and went through the door without looking back. Amanda stared after him for a long time before she turned over and closed her eyes with a sigh.

Chapter Seven

She opened her eyes to a shaft of midmorning sunlight that streamed across the fluffy bluc coverlet, and as her soft brown eyes stared at the ceiling, the memory of Jace's visit sent tingles of excitement all over her. She threw her legs over the edge of the bed and sat up, staring at the door, her face bright, her eyes brimming with excitement. Jace! Had it really happened? She touched her mouth and looked in the mirror, as if looking for evidence of the kisses he'd pressed against it. There was a faint bruise high on one arm, and she remembered with a thrill of pleasure the blaze of ardor she'd shared with him. It hadn't been a dream after all. But had he felt the same pleasure she had? Or had it all been something he already regretted in the cold light of day? Would he be different? Would he smile instead of scowl, would he be less antagonistic? Or would he hate her even more…?

She got into jeans and a scoop-necked powder-blue blouse and hurried downstairs, her hair loose and waving around her shoulders, her eyes full of dreams.

It was past ten o'clock, and she hadn't really expected Jace to be at the breakfast table, but she felt a surge of disappointment anyway when she opened the dining-room door and found only Marguerite and Terry there, Terry looking faintly irritated.

"There you are." He sighed. "Look, Mandy, you'll have to handle this account from here on in. Jackson called me a few minutes ago and he doesn't like the television spot we worked up—says it's too 'suggestive.'"

"But his son approved it," she protested.

"Without his permission, it seems," Terry grumbled. He gulped down the rest of his coffee and stood up. "Sorry to leave you like this, but if we lose that account we're in big trouble. It's the largest one we have—I don't need to remind you about that."

"No, of course not. Don't worry," she said with a smile, "I can take over here."

"I never did get to talk to Jace last night." He grinned back at her. "Maybe you'll have better luck." Then he thanked Marguerite for her hospitality, reminded Amanda to call him at the airport when she got into San Antonio after she finished discussing the account, and hurried away to get a cab.

"You don't sound quite as nervous of Jason as you did," Marguerite murmured, eyeing her with a mischievous gleam in her eyes. "I wonder why?"

Amanda flushed in spite of herself and burst out laughing. "I'll never tell," she murmured.

"I thought he'd get around to showing you how upset

he'd been," the older woman remarked as she stirred cream into her hot coffee. "I've never seen him like that. By the way," she added, glancing at Amanda, "I have a delightful surprise for you."

"What?" Amanda asked, all eyes.

"It will have to wait a little," came the mysterious reply, with a smile. "Jason's at the office this morning, but I think he may be in for lunch. Oh, and Duncan's at the dentist." She bit back a smile. "Jason loosened two of his caps."

Marguerite left minutes later for an arts council meeting, and Amanda took advantage of her absence to work on the presentation she planned to make to Jace. She hadn't much hope of his acceptance. He might enjoy making love to her, but she suspected he had a chauvinistic attitude toward women in business, and she was afraid he wouldn't even listen to her. It would be just like him.

Her mind kept going back to the things he'd said, to his explanation of the proposition he'd once made her. He'd actually been asking her to marry him all those years before. She sighed, closing her eyes at the thought. To be his wife, to have the right to touch him whenever she wanted, to run to him when he came home at night and throw herself into his arms, to look after him and see that he got enough rest, to plan her life around his, to buy things for him...she might have had all that, if only she'd been mature enough to realize it wasn't a proposition after all. She'd resented it all these years, and now there was nothing to resent; only something to regret with all her heart. Now she loved him, wanted him, needed him as only a woman could, and he was forever out of reach. He enjoyed the feel of her in his arms. But he still doubted her innocence, and he'd made it very clear he didn't have marriage in mind anymore. He simply wanted to sleep with her. Because now he had money, and she didn't. And he'd never be sure if she wanted him or the wealth she'd lost; he wouldn't take a chance by asking her to marry him again. She knew that.

She was so engrossed in her thoughts that she didn't hear the phone ring until the maid came and said it was for her.

She lifted the receiver on the phone by the sofa, wondering if Terry could be calling so soon after he'd left.

"Hello?" she murmured hesitantly.

"Hello, yourself," came Jace's reply in a voice like brown velvet. "What are you doing?"

"W-working on the ad presentation," she faltered.

"You don't sound very confident," he remarked. "If you don't believe in your own abilities, honey, how do you expect me to?"

"I do have confidence in the agency," she returned, her fingers trembling on the cord. "It's just that…I didn't expect you to call."

"Even after this morning?" he asked softly, and laughter rippled into the receiver. "I've got some nasty scratches on my back because of you."

She felt the heat rush into her cheeks as she remembered the way she'd dug her nails into him so hungrily. "It's your own fault," she whispered, smiling. "Don't make me take all the blame."

"Witch," he chuckled. "Come down to the office about eleven-thirty. I'll take you to lunch."

"I'd like that," she said softly.

"I know something I'd like better," he said bluntly.

"You lecherous man," she teased, feeling somewhat disoriented to hear him talking to her like this.

"Only with you, Miss Carson. You have such a delicious body. . . ."

"Jace!"

"Don't worry, it's not a party line." He laughed. "And my office is soundproof."

"Why?" she asked without thinking.

"So the rest of the staff won't hear the screams when I beat my secretary," he said matter-of-factly.

She burst out laughing. "Do you treat all your employees like that?"

"Only when they don't do as they're told," he returned. "Don't be late. I'm sandwiching you in between a board meeting and a civic club luncheon."

"A luncheon?" she asked. "But you shouldn't be having lunch with me…"

"I'll have coffee at the luncheon and tell them I'm on a diet."

"Nobody will believe that," she murmured. "Not as streamlined as you are."

"So you do notice me?"

"You're very attractive," she breathed, feeling her face flush again as she murmured the words.

There was a satisfied sound from the other end of the line. "Eleven-thirty. Don't forget," he said.

"I won't," she promised, and the line went dead.

She'd never been in the building before. It was a skyscraper in downtown Victoria, huge and imposing, with a fountain and greenery outside and huge trees in pots inside. Jace's office was on the fifth floor. She took the elevator up and walked across the large expanse of soft cream-colored carpet to his secretary's massive, littered desk.

"Is Jace…Mr. Whitehall in?" she asked nervously.

The secretary, a tall brunette with soft blue eyes, smiled at her. "Can't you hear the muffled roar?" she whispered conspiratorially, nodding toward the office, from which the rumble of Jace's deep angry voice was just audible. "A big real estate deal just fell through at the last minute and now Jace is trying to straighten out the mess. It's been something or other all morning long. Sorry, I didn't mean to cry all over you. Do you really want to see him?" she finished with wildly arched eyebrows.

"Oh, yes, I'm very brave," Amanda promised with a tiny grin.

"Angela, get me the file on the Bronson Corporation," Jace snapped over the intercom. "And let me know the minute Miss Carson gets here."

Angela looked at Amanda, who nodded, and spoke into the intercom, "She's here. Shall I send her in, or does she need something to stand behind?"

"Don't be cute, Miss Regan," he said.

She stepped into his office hesitantly, her heart racing, her eyes unsure as conflicting memories tore at her. He didn't look any different; his face was as hard as usual, his eyes giving nothing away in that narrow gaze that went from the V neck of her amber dress down the full skirt to her long tanned legs and her small feet encased in strappy beige sandals. But last night had seemed to be a turning point for Amanda, and she wondered if Jace really was as untouched by it as he seemed. If last night hadn't affected him, would he revert to the old antagonism and start taunting her as he had before? She clutched her purse nervously as the secretary smiled at her, winked and closed the door on her way out.

Jace was wearing a deep brown suit with a chocolate striped shirt and complementing tie, and his dark hair was just slightly ruffled, as if he'd been running an impatient hand through it. He looked so vibrantly masculine that she wanted to reach out and touch him, and that response frightened her.

"Thinking of running back out?" he asked quietly.

She shrugged her shoulders and smiled hesitantly. "Your secretary thought I might need a shield."

"Anyone else might. Not you." He got up and moved around the desk, his slow, graceful stride holding her gaze until he was standing just in front of her.

"Hi," she said softly, meeting his eyes with apprehension in her own.

He leaned his hands on either side of her against the door, trapping her, so close that she could feel the warmth of his tall, muscular body, catch the scent of his tangy, expensive cologne.

"Hi," he murmured, and something new was in his eyes, something she could barely define. Attraction, yes, perhaps even sensual hunger, but there was something else in that silvery gaze, too, and she couldn't decide exactly what it was.

He reached down and touched his cool, firm lips lightly to hers, drawing back just a breath to watch her.

"Just once," he murmured, "why don't you kiss me?"

She caught her breath at the idea of it, and the temptation was too great to resist. She clutched her small purse in one hand and held on to his sleeve with the other, going on tiptoe to press her lips softly against his.

He nipped at her lower lip with his teeth, a tantalizing, soft pressure that made her hungry. "You know what I like," he murmured under his breath.

She did, and almost without conscious effort, both arms went up around him while she nuzzled his mouth with hers to part his chiseled lips, letting the tip of her tongue trace, lightly, the long, slow curve of his mouth. Against her softness, she could feel the sudden heavy drum of his heart, hear the roughness of his breath.

"Like this, Jason?" she whispered against his mouth.

"Like this," he murmured, letting his body press her back against the smooth wood of the door, its hard contours fitting themselves expertly to hers. He crushed her soft mouth under his, taking control, the hunger in him almost tangible in the hot, tense silence that followed. A soft, strange sound whispered out of her throat as the madness burned into her mind, her body, and she felt the powerful muscles contract against her, the warmth of his body burning where it touched her in a long, aching caress.

He drew back a breath to look down at her flushed face, her passion-glazed eyes. "Now you know," he murmured in a husky deep tone.

"Know what?" she murmured blankly.

"Why the room is soundproof." He chuckled softly.

She flushed, dropping her eyes to his strong brown throat.

"What sweet little noises you make when I make love to you," he whispered against her forehead, easing the crush of his body. "It's good between us, Amanda. You're not a nervous little virgin anymore. You don't cringe away when I touch you. I like that."

If only he knew the truth! she thought with a twinge of pain at the words. She knew only what she'd learned from him.

He glanced at the thin gold watch on his wrist. "We'd

better go, if you don't want to be rushed through the first course. I've only got an hour."

"Are you sure you want to..." she began.

He bent and kissed her half-open mouth hard, springing back from the door in the same breath. "I'm sure. Hungry?"

She smiled shyly up at him. "Ravenous," she murmured.

He chuckled, glancing at her soft, slightly swollen mouth. "What an admission," he remarked, and laughed outright at the expression on her face. "Come on, honey, let's go."

"My lipstick!" she whispered as he started to open the door.

He studied her mouth. "You don't need it," he told her. "You're quite lovely enough without all that paint."

"That wasn't what I meant," she replied, staring up at him. "You've got it all over you."

He reached for his handkerchief, handed it to her and stood watching her intently while she wiped it away from his lips and cheek, his firm hands at her waist making her so nervous she fumbled slightly.

"Now," she murmured, handing him back the soiled handkerchief. "Your guilty secret is safe with me."

He chuckled deeply. "You little horror. What makes you think I feel guilty?"

"You didn't want anyone to see the lipstick," she reminded him. "I should have let you walk out there like that. It would have been an inspiration to your secretary."

"She doesn't kiss me," he told her.

She tried not to look too pleased. "She's very pretty," she murmured.

"Her boyfriend has a black belt in karate and he runs a very reputable newspaper," he told her.

She couldn't repress a grin. "Oh."

"Jealous of me, Mandy?" he asked, opening the door for her.

"Murderously," she whispered coquettishly, stepping out into the waiting room before he had time to get even.

He took her to a plush restaurant with burgundy carpeting and white linen tablecloths and horseshoe-shaped chairs upholstered with genuine leather. She ordered a chef's salad, jumping ahead of Jace before he could order for both of them, and he gave her a meaningful glare as he gave his own of steak and potatoes.

"I'm liberated," she smilingly reminded him when the waitress left.

He glowered at her, leaning back. "So am I. What about it?" he asked.

She laughed at that, her nervous fingers toying with her water glass. "I thought I'd irritated you."

"Honey, I'll admit that I think women look better in skirts than they do wearing pants, but I'll be the first to say that they are every bit as capable in business as men are."

That got her attention. Her lovely brown eyes opened wide. "I didn't realize you thought that way."

"I told you once, Amanda, you've never really known me at all," he remarked quietly.

"So it seems." She gripped the glass tighter. "Would you let me tell you why I think my ad agency could handle that Florida investment of yours and Duncan's?" she persisted.

"Go ahead."

"All right." She leaned forward on her forearms, watching the lights play on his dark hair. "You're developing a resort in inland Florida. It doesn't border on the ocean or the gulf, it isn't even on a river. It's near a large lake, though, and it's in a very picturesque area of central Florida surrounded by citrus groves and some cattle ranching. Why not let us plan a campaign around the retirement concept? It's in a perfect location," she went on, noticing the interest he was showing. "There's peace and quiet, and no resorts or tourist traps nearby to draw hordes of visitors every year. Since you're incorporating a shopping mall and gardens into the complex, it would be literally a city in itself. People are flocking to Arizona and places farther west than Texas to get sun and year-round peace and quiet along with it. Why not sell them serenity and natural beauty?"

He pursed his chiseled lips. "What kind of advertising did you have in mind?" he asked, and there was no condescension in his tone.

"You're planning to open the complex in six months, aren't you?" she asked, and he nodded. "Then this is the perfect time to do some feature material and work up ads for the more sophisticated magazines, those which appeal to an older, financially independent segment of the reading populace. There are two daily newspapers and three large radio stations, plus a weekly newspaper which all impact on the area where the complex is located. We'll do a multimedia ad campaign targeted to reach all those audiences. Then we'll get the figures on where the largest number of new Florida residents come from and send brochures to prominent real estate offices in those northern cities. We'll develop a theme for the complex, a logo, have a grand opening and get the governor or several politicians to make speeches, send invitations to the press, and—"

"Hold it!" He laughed, watching the excitement brighten her eyes. "Can I afford this saturation?"

She named a figure and both his eyebrows went up. "I hardly expected a figure that reasonable from you," he said bluntly.

Her eyes widened. "Why not?"

He shrugged. "I've already been approached by an ad agency out of New York." His eyes met hers. "The figure they named was several thousand more."

She snapped her fingers with a sigh. "Oh, drat!" she said with mock irritation.

He chuckled at that, but the smile quickly faded. "Who'd be handling the account, Amanda, you or your… partner?"

"Both of us," she replied. "Although I have the journalism degree," she added with a smile, "so I do most of the writing. Terry's forte is art and layout and mechanicals."

He blinked. "Mechanicals?"

"For the printer. Press-ready copy."

"And what if you launch this campaign and I don't sell condominiums?" he asked matter-of-factly.

"I throw myself under the wheels of your Mercedes while singing, 'What do I say, dear, after I say I'm sorry.'"

He reached for his drink with a faint smile playing on his chiseled lips.

"Well?" she asked impatiently.

He looked up and met her eye just as the waitress came toward them with a heavily laden tray. "I'll think about it and let you know at the party at the Sullevans'. Fair enough?"

She sighed. "Fair enough."

The meal was tantalizing; she hadn't realized until she started eating how hungry she was. She finished her salad, and refused dessert, lingering over thick, rich coffee while Jace attacked an enormous strawberry shortcake overflowing with fresh whipped cream.

"Calories, calories." She sighed, hating the sight of the delicious thing.

He smiled at her over his spoon. "I don't have to watch my waistlinc. I run it all off."

"I know. You work all the time."

"Not all the time," he reminded her with a pointed glance at her mouth.

She lowered her blushing face to her coffee cup.

Jace pulled into the parking lot behind the Whitehall building and followed Amanda's instructions to pull up short just in front of the small compact car she'd borrowed from Marguerite.

"Thank you for lunch," she said, "and for listening about the account."

"My pleasure, Miss Carson," he replied, his eyes searching her face quietly. "We'll take in a show at the Parisienne tonight. There's a trio there I think you'll enjoy, and we can dance."

Her heart leaped into her throat. "Me?" she whispered.

He leaned over and brushed his mouth tantalizingly against hers in a kiss just brief enough to leave her feeling empty when he drew away.

"You," he murmured gently. His eyes searched hers. "We're going to talk tonight."

"About what?" she asked dazedly.

"About you and me, honey," he replied curtly, "and

where we go from here. After what happened last night, I'm not going to let you run away again."

"But, Jace—"

"I don't have the time right now. Out you get, doe-eyes, I've got work to do. We'll talk about it tonight. Wear something sexy," he added with a wicked grin.

She opened the door and closed it, sticking out her tongue at him. He chuckled, waving as she put her car into gear and roared away.

Her spirits were soaring as she drove back to Casa Verde. What could Jace want to talk about? Marriage, perhaps? She drifted off into a delightful daydream, seeing herself in white satin and Jace in a tuxedo, standing before a minister in a church with stained-glass windows. If only! To marry Jace, to share his name, his home, his bed, his children...it would be the culmination of every dream she'd ever had. Of course, she reminded herself, he could be about to make a proposition of an altogether different kind. But she didn't think so. Jace's eyes had been too intent, his kisses too caring, for it to be only lust that he felt. No, he had something permanent in mind, he must have. Her eyes lit up like candles in dark room. How magical it would be if he loved her, too, if he felt the same devastating excitement that she felt when she was with him, touching him, holding him. Please, let it be, she prayed silently, let it be, let it be!

She pulled up at the entrance of Casa Verde and rushed up the steps, all the dreams shimmering in her eyes as she opened the front door.

"Is that you, dear?" Marguerite called. "In the living room!"

She followed the voice, her mouth open to tell Marguerite what a lovely lunch she'd had with Jason, when she saw the second person in the room.

"See? I told you I had a surprise for you!" Marguerite exclaimed, her dark eyes lighting up merrily.

"Hello, darling," Beatrice Carson greeted her daughter, rising in a cloud of amber chiffon to float across the room, her blond hair in a high coiffure, her soft brown eyes full of love and laughter.

Amanda allowed herself to be embraced and fussed over, numbly, her mind spinning off into limbo as she realized the problems this was going to create.

Things had been going so beautifully. Jason had been so different. And now Bea was here, and all the lovely dreams were shredding. Jason would think she'd sent for her mother—he'd never believe that Marguerite had done it. He'd be furious, because he hated Amanda's mother. He always had.

"Well, don't you want to know why I'm here?" Bea asked in her lovely soft voice.

"Uh, why are you here, Mother?" Amanda asked obligingly.

"I'm getting married, darling! You're going to have a father!" Bea gushed.

Amanda sat down. She had to. It was too much, too soon. "Married?"

"Yes, darling," her mother said, sitting down beside her to catch her hands and hold them tightly. Bea's fingers were cold, and Amanda knew she was nervous. "To Reese Bannon. He asked me two days ago, and I said yes. You'll like him. He's a very strong man, very capable, and you can come and stay with us whenever you like."

"But…why have you come to Casa Verde?" Amanda breathed.

"Marguerite kindly offered to help me pick out my trousseau and plan the wedding," Bea replied with a beaming smile. "And I knew you'd want to be included as well. It's going to be a small affair, in Nassau, and we're having a reception afterward at the house. It's lovely, dear. He calls it Sea Jewel and it has its own private beach with lots of sea grape trees and poincianas and the water is such an incredible green and blue and aqua all mixed and sparkling…you'll simply love it!"

"When are you getting married, Mother?" Amanda asked, just beginning to realize that Reese would inherit the responsibility for her mother and her mother's debts.

"Next week!" Bea sighed. "I wanted more time, but Reese was simply adamant, so I gave in. I'm so excited!"

"Yes, so am I." Amanda smiled, pressing her mother's fingers. Bea was such a child, so full of ups and downs, so sparkling bright, like an amber jewel. Amanda couldn't help loving her, even while she blanched at some of her escapades and spending sprees.

"Mother, about the trousseau…we don't have very much in the bank…" Amanda began cautiously.

"Oh, I'm buying the trousseau—it's my wedding gift," Marguerite said with a happy sigh. "I can't wait to get started. Bea, we simply must go to Saks tomorrow morning early. There's so little time…!"

"Yes, indeed," Bea agreed, and launched into the reception plans.

Amanda sat beside her, listening, smiling now and then at her mother's exuberance, and only going upstairs when the afternoon had drifted away to change for supper and worry about Jace's reaction. She had a horrible premonition that he wasn't going to be at all pleased.

She dressed carefully in a becoming gray skirt with an embroidered pink blouse, noting with pleasure the way it molded her slender body. The fit was perfect, and though the clothes were two years old, they didn't show it. Amanda took excellent care of her wardrobe, making innovative alterations to keep it up to date. A scarf here, some jewelry there, the addition of a stylish blouse to an old but classic suit made all the difference. Shoes had been a problem at first, but she quickly learned to buy at the end of the season, when prices were slashed. She never bought anything except during sales. She couldn't afford to.

She was just running a brush through her long hair when there was a slight tap on the door and her mother came in, vividly captivating in a pale pink dress that highlighted her rosy complexion and exquisitely coiffed hair.

"I thought we might go downstairs together," Bea suggested softly. "I...well, I know Jason doesn't like me, and he's much less likely to say something if I'm with you," she added with a nervous smile. "You haven't told him about the bull, have you, darling?"

"No, Mother," Amanda replied soothingly. She put down the brush and hugged her petite mother. "I'm so glad you've found someone. I know how lonely you've been these last few years."

"Not so very lonely, my dear," Bea replied. She touched her daughter's cheek. "I had you, after all."

Amanda smiled. "We had each other."

Bea nodded. She studied her daughter's face intently. "Marguerite said that you and Jason are...softening toward one another. Is that so?"

Amanda blushed fiercely and turned away. "I'm not sure. I don't know if he even likes me."

"Amanda..." Bea bit her lower lip. "Dear, I've often wondered if all that arguing between you wasn't really an indication of something much deeper than dislike. You've shied away from Jason for many years. I'd like to think it wasn't because of my quite ridiculous attitude toward him when you were in your teens. I was a dreadful snob. I only wish I'd realized it at the time, before the damage was done."

"What damage?"

"Between you and Jace." Bea studied the carpet. "Amanda, men like Jason Whitehall are very rare creatures. The man's man isn't popular these days. Women much prefer softer men who cry and hurt and make mistakes and apologize on bended knee, and that's all very well, I suppose. It's a new world, a new generation, with new and better ideas of what life should be." Her eyes were wistful for a moment. "But men like Jason are a breed apart. They make their own rules and they don't bend. A woman who's lucky enough to be loved by a man like that is...blessed." She drew a long, quiet sigh. "Oh, Mandy, don't run from him if you love him," she burst out. "Don't let the rift I've caused between you blind you to Jason's good qualities. I lost my happiness, but you still have a chance for yours."

"Mother, I don't understand what you're saying," Amanda whispered blankly.

"You're such a good girl, my dear," Bea murmured, her eyes sad and full of vanished dreams. "But it takes so much more than noble intentions with some men...."

"Bea, are you in there?" Marguerite called.

Bea looked faintly irritated. "Yes, dear, we're coming!"

She patted Amanda's arm. "I'll try to explain it to you later. I must tell you something, a secret I've kept from you. We'll talk later, all right?"

"Yes, darling," Amanda replied with a puzzled smile. "Let's go down."

They were sitting in the living room, waiting for dinner to be served, when Jason came in from the office. He looked tired and out of sorts, his silver eyes glittering in a face that showed every day of its age.

He caught sight of Bea as soon as he entered the room, and he seemed to explode.

"What the hell are you doing here?" he asked the stunned woman. His eyes shot to Amanda's white face. "A little premature, wasn't it, calling Mama? I don't remember making any promises."

Amanda started to speak, but Bea was quicker. "I invited myself," she told him, rising like a little blond wraith to face him bravely. "I'm getting married, Jason. I came to invite my daughter to the wedding."

"Oh, you're marrying this one?" he asked cuttingly, his eyes openly hating her. "Will you be as faithful to him as you were to that poor damned fool you married last time?"

"Jason, where are your manners?" Marguerite burst out. "Bea's my friend!"

"Like hell she is," Jason replied coldly, eyeing Beatrice, and Amanda saw her mother's face go sheet-white.

"What are you talking about?" Marguerite persisted.

"Ask your...friend," Jason growled. "She knows, don't you, Mrs. Carson?" He emphasized the "Mrs.," making an insult of it.

"Leave my mother alone," Amanda said, standing. Her

eyes fenced with his. "You've no right to insult her like that. You don't know her."

"Honey, I know more about her than you'd believe," he replied with a cold smile. "Remind me to tell you one day. It'll open your eyes."

"You…you…cowboy!" Amanda threw at him, her lower lip trembling, her eyes bright with tears.

"That sounds more like old times," he told Amanda, something like a shadow passing over his face. "I like it better when you drop the pretense. I told you once, and I'll tell you again, you aren't getting your hands on my money." He glanced harshly at Bea. "And you might as well send Mama home. I'm not financing her wedding. And neither are you, Mother," he informed Marguerite coldly. "If you so much as try to buy that well-heeled slut a handkerchief at any department store in town, I'll close down every account you've got." He turned on his heel and walked out the door, his spine rigid with dislike and temper.

Marguerite threw her arms around Bea. "Oh, my dear, I'm so sorry! I don't know what's the matter with him!"

Bea wept like a child, tears running down her cheeks. Amanda put her arms around her, taking her from Marguerite, and held her tight.

"It's all right, Mama," she cooed, as she had so many times. "It's going to be all right."

But even as she said it, she knew better. Her world was upside down, Jace hated her again, and she only wished she knew why. Could he really hold a grudge so long, from childhood, and hate Beatrice for something she'd said to him years ago? Why did he hate her so passionately! And why in the world did he call her a slut? Heaven knew, Bea might be a lot of things, but that wasn't one of them. She was so proper, always socially correct. She would never dream of soiling her reputation with an extramarital affair. Amanda rocked Bea gently, her eyes meeting Marguerite's pained ones over the thin shoulder. Jace could be so cruel. Her eyes closed. How could he say such things after the passion that had burned between them like a wildfire out of control? She'd thought that he might care for her, especially after the New York trip, after the kisses they'd shared. But he hadn't cared. He didn't care. And how was she going to protect her fragile mother from his unreasonable hatred? She felt like crying herself. The day had begun with such promise, only to end in desolation.

The three women sat down to supper without Jace, who came back downstairs an hour later dressed in brown slacks, a tweed jacket and a white roll-neck shirt. He walked out of the house without a word, probably on his way to see Tess, Amanda guessed.

"Don't look so tragic, darling," Bea said gently, sensing her daughter's depression. "It will all work out. Things do, you know."

Amanda tried to smile. "Of course they will," she agreed numbly.

"I could just strangle my son," Marguerite said under her breath, stabbing viciously at a piece of steak on her plate. "Of all the colossal gall...!"

"Don't, dear," Bea pleaded, touching her friend's manicured hand lightly. "Jace can't help the way he feels about me, and there is some justification. After all..." She bit her lip jerkily. "After all," she tried again with a pained glance at Amanda, "it was I who ran into his bull, not Amanda. She wasn't even driving."

Marguerite's eyes widened. "You? But Amanda said..."

"She was trying to protect me. No." Bea sighed miserably. "That's not true. I begged her to protect me. Knowing how Jace dislikes me, I was afraid he'd deny me the hospitality of Casa Verde, so I let poor Amanda take the blame for it all...to my shame," she finished weakly. Her lovely dark eyes misted with tears as she looked at her shocked daughter. "I know I've been a trial to you, my dear. I seem to have walked around in a trance since your...since your father's death."

"That doesn't give Jason the right to call you foul names," Marguerite interrupted, her own dark eyes blazing. "I think it's outrageous and as soon as he calms down, I'm going to tell him so."

Amanda couldn't help the brief smile that twitched her lips. Marguerite was no braver than she when it came to facing Jace's fiery temper.

The next day passed in a foggy haze, with Bea and Amanda cautiously keeping close to Marguerite's side and avoiding Jace as much as possible. He managed to find plenty to keep him busy around the ranch and at his office, but the eyes that occasionally glanced Amanda's way were icy gray, cold. It was as if that magical night had never happened, as if he'd never touched her with tenderness. And Bea, for all her usual gaiety, seemed crushed, almost guilty. Reese Bannon had promised to wire her the money for her trousseau, despite Marguerite's protests that she wanted the privilege of buying it. The two older women spent most of the day shopping, while Amanda kept to her room and mourned for what might have been.

Bea and Marguerite went to visit a mutual friend that evening after supper, and Amanda returned to her room to change into slacks and a blouse. When she went back down, wandering out onto the darkened porch to enjoy the cool peace of evening, a movement caught her eye and made her start. She'd reached the big rocking chair at the side of the porch when a quiet figure detached itself from the swing and stood up.

"Don't run away," Jace said quietly. "I'm not armed."

She hated the bitterness in his deep voice. The very sound of it was like an ache in her soul. She could hardly bear to be near him after the harsh accusations he'd made. But she sat down in the huge, bare wood rocker and leaned back. The woven cane made a soft, creaking sound as she began to rock. The sound, combining with the murmur of crickets and frogs, was a wild lullaby in the sweet-scented darkness.

"I didn't think you'd be at home," she remarked coolly.

"Obviously, or you'd still be hiding in your room," he said curtly.

She leaned her head back against the rocking chair, gazing out into the darkness. Jace made her feel like a tightly wound rubber band. She felt as remote from him as the moon when he drew into himself like this.

"You sat out here with me once before on a moonless night," he remarked suddenly, his voice deep and quiet in the stillness. "Remember, Amanda?"

"The night your father died," she recalled, feeling again the emptiness of the rooms without Judge Whitehall's domineering presence, the weeping of Marguerite and Bea… "We didn't say two words."

He laughed shortly. "You sat beside me and held my hand. Nothing more than that. No tears or wailing, or promises of comfort. You just sat and held my hand."

"It was all I could think to do," she admitted. "I knew how deeply you cared about him…even more than Duncan did, I think. You aren't an easy man to offer comfort to, Jason. Even then I expected you to freeze me out, or tell me to go away. But you didn't."

"Men don't like being vulnerable, honey, didn't you know?" he asked in a strangely gentle tone, and she remembered another time when he'd made a similar remark. "I wouldn't have let anyone else near me that night, Amanda, not even Mother, do you know that? You've always managed to get close when I'd have slapped anyone else away." He shifted. "I'd let you bandage a cut that I wouldn't let a doctor touch."

She felt her heart pounding. Watch out, she reminded herself, this is just a game to him, and he's a master player. Don't let him hurt you.

She stood up with a jerky motion. "I'd better go in. It's getting late."

"Amanda, talk to me!" he growled.

"About what?" she managed tearfully. "About my mother? About myself? We're sluts, you said so, and you know everything, don't you, Jason God Almighty Whitehall!"

She turned and ran for the front door, hearing his harsh, muffled curse behind her.

More restless than ever the next morning, Amanda wandered down to the stable to look at a new snowy-white Arabian foal. It brought back memories of the old days on her father's ranch when she'd spent hours watching the newborn foals, never tiring of their amusing antics. This one was a colt, on wobbly little legs that looked far too long for him.

She was so involved in the sight of the colt and his mother

that she didn't hear the sound of approaching horses' hooves. She did hear the rapidly nearing footsteps a moment later, though, and turned just in time to see Jace coming down the wide aisle, his booted feet sinking into the fresh, honey-colored woodchips that covered the floor.

He moved with a slow, easy grace that was as much a part of him as that worn black Stetson pulled low on his forehead. She loved the very sight of him, but she turned away from it, hurting all over again at his insults, his rejection.

"All alone?" he asked curtly. "Where's brother Duncan this morning?"

"At the office," she said tightly.

"And the others?" he added, refusing to even speak Bea's name.

"Gone to town shopping." She glared at him. "And not to spend your money."

He ignored that, watching the colt. "Not afraid of me, kitten?"

"Or of twenty like you," she shot back, turning away, too proud to let her very real apprehension show.

She leaned over the stall gate and stared down at the colt, who was suckling his mother. The white mare stood with her ears pricked and alert, watching the humans closely.

Jace moved to the gate beside her, so close that his arm touched hers where it rested on the rough wood, and a sweet, reckless surge of delight filled her.

"Do you still show them?" she asked, hoping to change the subject.

"I don't have time, honey," he said, and his voice was no longer angry. "The Johnsons' daughter enters one or two a year on the horse show circuit, and I've got a few trophies from bygone days, but most of my stock is at stud. I let Johnson handle the show circuit. All I do is take credit for the trophies."

She feathered a glance at him, amazed at the humorous note in his voice. "Who shows you?" she asked lightly, surprising him.

He raised an eyebrow at her and shoved his hat back over his dark, unruly hair. "Daring, aren't you?"

She shook back her silvery-blond hair until it drifted around her shoulders in a cloud. "I like to live dangerously once in a while," she agreed.

He flicked her cheek with a lean finger. "Not on my land," he cautioned. "I wouldn't want to be responsible for you getting hurt." He cut a hard gaze down at her, holding her eyes deliberately in a heady silence.

Her lips parted slightly from the shock of it, and his eyes caught the movement, darting to the soft pink mouth with unnerving quickness.

She fought down the longing to move closer to him, to feel his hard body against hers, to tempt his mouth into violence…having experienced the skill of that beautiful mouth, she was unbearably hungry for it. She tore her eyes away from his and struggled to control her quick, unsteady breathing.

"The, uh, the foal is lovely," she said unsteadily.

He moved closer, coming up behind her to make retreat impossible, his muscular arms resting on the gate on either side of her to imprison her there. His body was warm, and she could feel its heat, smell the tangy cologne he used drifting down into her nostrils.

"Do…you have any more?" she continued when he didn't answer her.

She felt his breath in her hair. "You smell of wildflowers," he murmured sensuously.

"It's my shampoo," she whispered inanely.

He shifted, bringing her body into slight, maddening contact with his. She could feel his powerful legs touching hers, his broad chest at her shoulder blades.

"How many Arabians do you have now?" she asked in a high, unfamiliar voice.

"Enough," he murmured, bending to nuzzle aside the hair at her neck and press his warm, open mouth to the quivering tender flesh he found under it.

"Jason!" she gasped involuntarily.

His chest rose and fell heavily against her back. His mouth moved up, nibbling at her ear, her temple. "God, your skin is soft," he whispered huskily. "Like velvet. Satin."

Her fingers gripped the gate convulsively while she fought for control and lost. Her throat felt as if there were rocks in it.

Even while she was protesting, her body was melting back against his, yielding instinctively.

His hands moved, gripping her tiny waist painfully.

"Oh, Jason, you mustn't!" she managed in a hoarse plea. "Not after all the things you've said!" she accused, hating him for what he could do to her.

"I don't give a damn what I said," he growled in a haunted tone. "I want you so much, I ache with it!"

She struggled, but he whipped her around and pinned her against the gate with the carefully controlled weight of his body. His eyes burned down into hers, his face taut with longing.

Tears of intense emotion welled in the wide brown eyes that pleaded with him. Her soft hands pressed against the unyielding hardness of his chest.

"Are these games really necessary?" he asked curtly. "I know what I do to you. I can feel it. Do you have to pretend? I don't mind if you're experienced, damn it—it doesn't matter!"

She shoved against him furiously, only to find herself helpless in those hurting, powerful hands. "Let me go, Jason Whitehall!" she blurted out. "I'm not experienced, I'm not easy and I'm not pretending!"

His nostrils flared as he held her rigid body. "Do you expect me to believe that? My God, you were wild in my arms, as hungry for it as I was."

"I don't sleep around!" she exclaimed.

"Your mother does," he returned fiercely.

She glared at him. "More of your unfounded slander, cowboy?"

His eyes glittered dangerously. "I found her in my father's bedroom," he fired back, contempt in every hard line of his face. "A month before he died. She was still married to that poor, cold fish of a father of yours."

Her face went stone-white. It was unthinkable that Bea would have behaved like that with Jude Whitehall! He was lying, he had to be! But there wasn't any trace of deception in his expression. He meant it!

"My mother?" she breathed incredulously.

"Your mother," he returned coldly. "The only consolation was that no one knew—not Duncan, especially not my mother. But I did," he added gruffly. "And every time I saw her, I wanted to wring her soft neck!"

She licked her lips, feeling their dryness with a sense

of unreality. "It wasn't because she snubbed you," she whispered, knowing the truth now.

"No. It was because she was carrying on an affair with my father, and I couldn't stop it. All I could do was try to protect my mother. I did that, but your mother took years off his life. She robbed us all."

She lowered her eyelids wearily. It was the last straw. And she had never even suspected!

"And you think I'm like her," she whispered. "That was why you assumed I was sleeping with Terry."

"Something like that." He laughed shortly. "You don't think it was because I was jealous?"

She shook her head with a bitter little smile. "That would never occur to me." She drew in a deep, ragged breath. "I'll pack and leave today."

His hands tightened, hurting. "Not yet. What about your precious account? Your *partner* won't be pleased if you let it slip through your fingers."

Her eyes flew open, tormented and hurting. "Why don't you just shoot me?" she asked, tears in her eyes. "You've made life hell for me for so long…and Mother and her spending sprees…now you tell me…she was cheating on my father…oh, God, I wish I was dead!"

Panic-stricken, mad with wounded pride and betrayal, she broke away from him with a surge of maniacal strength, and ran outside. Catching sight of Jace's horse tethered by the door, she vaulted into the saddle before he could stop her. Ignoring his curt command to rein in, she leaned forward, over the silky gray mane, and gave the spirited horse its head, blindly hanging on as they plunged into the nearby forest and kept going.

The animal reacted to its rider's emotional upheaval by

putting on a frantic burst of speed and going too close under a low-hanging limb. Amanda, with some inner warning, looked up through tear-blinded eyes, but she was too late to save herself. The limb came straight at her, and she felt the rough scrape of wood, the jar of impact, just before a numbness sent her plummeting down into a strange darkness.

Chapter Eight

Duncan was sitting beside her when she opened her eyes to blazing sunlight, medical apparatus and a wicked headache.

"I won't ask the obvious question," she said weakly, and tried to smile. "But I would like to know who clubbed me."

Duncan smiled back, pressing the slender hand lying on top of the crisp white hospital sheet. "A pecan limb, actually," he said. "You didn't duck."

"I didn't have time." She felt her forehead and touched her throbbing brow, aware of painful bruising all over her body. "Have I been here long?"

"Overnight," he replied. "Jace's been pacing the halls like a madman, muttering and being generally abusive to every member of the hospital staff who came within snarling distance."

Jace! It all came back. The argument, the accusation

he'd made, her own shock at finding out, finally, the reason he hated her and Bea so much. Her dark eyes closed.

Duncan watched her closely, frowning slightly. "What did he say to you, Mandy?" he asked quietly.

"Nothing," she lied.

"Don't lie to me," he said without malice. "You've never done it before. He hurt you, didn't he?"

"What happened was between Jace and me," she told him. Her wan, drawn face made a smile for him. "I could just as easily have fallen off. I ran into a limb, that's all."

"He acts guilty as hell," he said, studying her. "Like a hunted man. He's been in and out of here six times already, just looking at you."

"I'm not telling you anything, Duncan. You might as well give up."

He sighed angrily. "Your mother will be by later," he said finally, giving in, but with reluctance. "She was here earlier."

"When can I go home?"

He shrugged. "They want to do some more tests."

"I don't need any more tests," she said stiffly, already crumpling under visions of a mountainous hospital bill that her meagre insurance wouldn't pay.

Duncan read her worried expression accurately. "Don't start worrying about money," he told her. "The bill is our responsibility."

"The devil it is!" she burst out, sitting up so fast she almost fell off the bed. She pushed back her straggly hair, and her dark eyes burned. "Oh, no, Duncan, I'm not having Jason Whitehall throw another debt up to me."

He caught on to that immediately. "What debt has he been throwing up to you?" he asked sharply.

She flushed, and averted her gaze to the venetian blinds letting slitted beams of sunlight into the cheery yellow room.

"How nice of you to come and visit me, Duncan," she said sweetly. "When can I go home?" she asked again.

He sighed with exasperation. "I'll ask the doctor, all right?"

"Tell him I said I'm leaving in the morning, and he can take his tests and..." she began.

"Now, now," he said soothingly. He reached over and pushed the hair away from her forehead. "God, you're going to have a bruise there!" he murmured.

"Purple, I hope," she said lightly. "I've got a gorgeous cotton frock with purple flowers. It'll be a perfect match."

"You—" he grinned "—are incorrigible."

"Oh, being slammed in the head by trees does wonders for me," she agreed saucily, smiling up at him from her pillow.

He stuck his hands in the pockets of his beige trousers, shaking his dark head. "I wouldn't recommend trying it too often," he said. "You could have too much of a good thing."

She lifted a hand to her forehead and winced. "You can say that again. How's Jace's horse, by the way?"

"Fine," he replied. "Thanks to you. He didn't hit his head."

She started to answer him, but the door swung open and Jace walked in. He was still in a nasty temper. It showed in the hard lines of his face, his blazing darkened silver eyes. But he looked haggard, too, as if he hadn't slept. His dark brown roll-neck sweater and cream-colored slacks looked rumpled, as well. And his hair was tousled, as if his hands had worried it.

Amanda stiffened involuntarily, looking vaguely like a small wild creature in a trap. Jace's sharp gaze didn't miss the expression that flitted across her pale features, and it tightened his jaw.

"How are you?" he asked curtly.

"Just dandy, thanks," she said with bravado. She even smiled, although her eyes were like dead wood.

"The doctor said you had a close call," he added quietly, ignoring Duncan. "If you'd been sitting a fraction of an inch higher in the saddle, you'd have broken your damned neck."

"Sorry to disappoint you," she said in a ghostly voice, her lower lip trembling with the hurt she felt as she met his cold, unfeeling gaze.

He turned away, glaring at Duncan. "I thought you had a meeting with Donavan on that Garrison contract."

Duncan bristled, one of the few times Amanda had ever seen him stand up to Jace. "The contract can damned well wait. Maybe you can turn off your emotions, but I can't. I was worried about Amanda."

"She looks spry enough to me," he bit off.

"Easy words for the man who put her in the hospital!" Duncan threw at him.

Jace's eyes exploded. He moved toward Duncan, checking himself immediately with that iron control that was part of him. His eyes shifted to Amanda, blaming, accusing, but she only lifted her chin and stared back at him.

"I put myself here, Duncan," she said with quiet dignity. "Don't blame your brother for that."

"Since when did I ask you to defend me?" Jace demanded hotly.

She dropped her eyes to the green hospital gown with its rounded neckline showing above the sheet that was drawn up to her waistline. She only had two gowns with her on this trip, neither of which was suitable to be seen in. She was glad no one had bothered to bring one for her to wear.

"God forbid that I should stand up for you," she said in a husky whisper, feeling the whip of the words even through the daze of drugs and the headache.

"Why don't you go back to the ranch and fuss over your damned horse?" Duncan asked shortly. "He's part of the blood stock, remember, worth far more than a mere woman!"

"How would you like to step outside with me?" Jace asked in a goaded tone.

"Please!" Amanda pleaded, holding her head as the pain swept a wave of nausea over her. "Please don't fight. Both of you, just go away and let me groan in peace."

"Can I bring you anything?" Duncan said tightly.

She shook her head, refusing to open her eyes and look at either one of them. "I'll be fine. Just tell them I'm checking out in the morning, if you don't mind, Duncan."

"You'll check out when the doctor says so, and not one minute before," Jace told her curtly.

"I will check out when I decide to," she replied, opening her eyes and sitting up straight in the bed to glare across the room at him. "I am not a woman of means anymore, as you so frequently remind me. I am one of the nation's deprived, and that goes for insurance as well as wardrobe. I cannot afford," she said deliberately, "to enjoy the hospitality of this lovely white hotel longer than one full day or I will be paying off the bill in my dotage. I am leaving tomorrow. Period."

"Like hell," Jace shot back. His face went rigid. "I'll take care of the bill."

"No!" she burst out, eyes blazing. "I will gladly starve to death before I'll let you buy me a soda cracker! I hate you!"

A shadow passed across his face, but not a trace of expression showed on it. He turned without another word and went out the door.

"Whew," Duncan breathed softly. "Talk about having the last word..."

"Are you going to argue with me, too?" she grumbled.

"Not me, darling." He laughed. "I'm not up to your weight."

She nodded. "I'm glad you noticed." She smiled.

"I only wish I knew what was going on between you and my brother," he added narrowly.

She avoided his eyes. She couldn't tell him about the terrible accusation Jace had made. She couldn't do that to Duncan, who'd stood by her for so long, against such odds. Her weary eyes closed. Jace could hate her and it didn't matter, not anymore. She was tired of writhing under his contempt, tired of aching for him. At least when he was hating her he wouldn't look close enough to see how desperately she loved him.

Less than an hour later Bea came in, her face terribly pale, her eyes troubled. She hugged Amanda gently, tears rolling down her cheeks, her normally faultless coiffure looking unkempt. She sank down into a deep, padded chair by the bed and held Amanda's hand tightly.

"I've been so worried," she confessed. "I feel responsible."

Amanda stared at her. "Mother! Why should you feel guilty? It was my fault."

"Duncan says you argued with Jason," Bea said doggedly. "And I'll bet it was about me. It was, wasn't it, darling?"

Amanda dropped her eyes to the small, thin-skinned hand clasping her own. "Yes." She sighed wearily, too weak to pretend anymore.

"About me...and his father," Bea suggested hesitatingly.

Amanda nodded without raising her eyes.

Bea sighed, worrying her lower lip with her teeth. "I'd hoped you'd never have to be told," she whispered. "I was sure that Jason knew, but I hoped..." Her dark eyes met her daughter's, and they were bright with pain. "I loved him, Amanda," she whispered tearfully. "He was everything Jason is, and more. A man who could carry the world on his shoulders and never strain. I hated what I was doing, even then, but I was helpless. I'd have gone to him on my deathbed if he'd called me." She brushed away a stray tear. "I loved your father, Amanda, I did. But there was no comparison between that love and what I felt for Jude. I hurt your father, and Marguerite, very much, and I'll always be sorry for that. But as long as I live, I'll remember the way it was when Jude held me. I'll cherish those crumbs of memory like a miser with a treasure until I die, and I can't apologize. He was the air I breathe."

Amanda stared at her blankly, her lips trembling, trying to form words. When Jace had made his accusation, it had been so easy to deny it. But now she had to face the truth. Bea was revealing a love as powerful as that Amanda felt for Jace. She studied her mother's delicate features, and saw for the first time the deep sadness lurking in her eyes. How would it be if Jace were married? Would she feel any less deeply about him? And if he wanted her, would she be able to deny him, loving him? It was so easy to pass moral judgment…until you found yourself in the shoes of the judged.

"You feel that way about Jace, don't you?" Bea asked gently, her gaze intent.

Amanda nodded, smiling bitterly. "For all the good it will ever do me. He only wants me, Mother, he doesn't love me."

"With Jude, it was one and the same thing," Bea said quietly. "I imagine his son is no different. But you have an advantage that I didn't, my darling. Jace isn't married."

"He hates me," came the sad reply. "It hasn't stopped him from wanting me, but he hates what he feels."

Bea's small fingers contracted. "Perhaps you'll have to take the first step toward him," she said gently, with a tiny smile. "Amanda, nothing is as important as love. Nothing. Those few weeks I had when Jude was the sun in my sky are as precious as diamonds to me. Nothing can ever take away the memory of them. I keep him here, now," she whispered, touching the soft fabric over her breast, "with me always, wherever I go. I care for Reese Bannon, in the same fond way that I cared for your father. I can be happy with him. But Jude was the love of my life, as Jace is the love of yours. I had no chance at all, Amanda. My happiness was built on the crumbling dreams of another woman. But you have the chance. Don't throw it away for pride, my darling. Life is so very short."

Amanda pressed the small hand holding hers, and tears welled in her eyes. She hadn't realized that her mother was a woman, with all a woman's hopes and needs. Perhaps all Bea's mad sprees were her way of rebelling against a life too confining, dreams unrealized. She was childlike in a sense, but such a sad, lonely child. Remembering Jude Whitehall, how closely his son resembled him, Amanda could even understand Bea's passion for him. She could understand it very well.

"I love you," she whispered to her mother.

Bea sniffed through her tears. "I'm a weak person," she whispered brokenly with a tiny smile.

Amanda shook her head. "Just a loving woman. If Jace loved me back, it wouldn't matter if he had ten wives—I wouldn't be able to stop my feet from taking me to him. I do love him so!"

Bea moved onto the bed and gathered her daughter into her frail arms. "Hush, baby," she whispered, as she had when Amanda had been small and hurt. "Mama's here. It's going to be all right, now, you'll see. Everything is going to be all right."

Amanda closed her eyes and let the tears come. She hadn't felt so close to Bea since her childhood.

She got up the next morning, dressed while holding on to the bed for support, and ran a brush through her hair. Marguerite came in to find her sitting quietly on the edge of the big reclining chair in the corner, looking pale and fragile and terribly vulnerable. The only clothes she had to put on were those she'd been wearing when she had the accident—the same jeans and white top. They were dirty and stained, but at least she was out of the shapeless hospital gown and wearing what belonged to her.

"My dear, you aren't really going to try and go back to the ranch so soon, are you?" Marguerite asked gently.

"I'm going home," she said in a small voice. She barely

looked able to sit up. "All the way home. I've got the bus fare. I know Mother wants me to stay and help her plan the wedding, but I just can't. She'll understand."

The older woman sighed. "I was afraid you'd say that, so I took the necessary precautions. I do hope you'll forgive me someday."

Amanda blinked. She felt faintly nauseated, and her head was swimming. Marguerite's words didn't register at first, until the door opened and Jace walked in, very elegant in gray slacks and a patterned gray-and-tan sports jacket over an open-necked white shirt.

"She wants to take a bus home," Marguerite said with compassionate amusement, turning her dark eyes on her son. "Just as I expected."

Jace moved forward, and Amanda jerked backward as he reached her. Something—a faint movement in his face—almost registered in her whirling mind, but she stared up at him resentfully.

"Where's Duncan?" she asked apprehensively.

"At work," Jace said harshly. "Where I should be."

"Jace!" Marguerite exclaimed.

"I didn't ask you to come," she said through numb lips, glaring up at him. "I can get home all by myself."

His nostrils flared, his eyes glittered. "Brave words," he said curtly.

Her eyes dropped to his brown throat, and she felt all the fight go out of her in a long, weary sigh. Her body wasn't up to it. She slumped in the chair. "Yes," she whispered, "very brave. I hurt so," she moaned, dropping her aching head into her hands as hot tears stung her eyes.

Jace reached down and lifted her in his hard arms, holding her clear of the floor.

"Don't," she whimpered. "They have wheelchairs...."

"And I don't have all day to wait for them to bring one," he growled. "Let's go, Mother."

Marguerite followed them out into the hall, muttering at Jace's broad back.

"I've already signed you out," Jace said quietly. "And if you say one word about the bill," he added, glaring into her eyes from a distance of bare inches, "I'll give you hell, Amanda."

Her eyes closed, making the wild sensations she felt in his warm, hard arms even more sensuous. "When have you ever given me anything else?" she whispered.

"When have you let me?"

The question was soft and deep, and it shocked her into opening her eyes and looking straight up into his. The impact of it went right through her body. She couldn't drag her gaze away from his. It stimulated her pulse, stifled her breath in her body. Her sharp nails involuntarily dug into his shoulder.

They were outside now, in the parking lot, and Marguerite had gone around the Mercedes to unlock the passenger side.

Jace's eyes dropped to Amanda's soft, parted mouth. "Sharp little claws," he whispered, and Marguerite was too far away to hear. "And I know just how much damage they can do."

She gasped, shaken by his reference to those moments of intimacy they had shared. His arms drew her imperceptibly closer before he walked around the car with her. "Shocked, Amanda?" he asked quietly.

She grasped at sanity. "Scarlet women don't get shocked," she reminded him shakily.

"I'm beginning to wonder if my first impression wasn't more accurate than my second," he replied in a low tone. His eyes sought hers. "Was it, Amanda?"

"I don't know what your first impression was," she reminded him.

"Pretty devastating, little one," he said under his breath. He slid her in onto the back seat of the small car while Marguerite held the door open for him and then turned to get into the passenger seat.

Amanda met Jace's narrow eyes from a distance of scant inches as he put her down, so close that she could smell the aftershave he'd used clinging to his darkly tanned face.

He drew away in a matter of seconds, although it seemed as if time had stopped while they stared at one another, and her eyes involuntarily clung to his tall figure while he went around the car and got behind the wheel.

"Dear, are you sure you're up to going home with us?" Marguerite asked worriedly. She half turned with one elegantly clad arm over the back of the seat to study the younger woman. "You look so pale."

"I'm fine," Amanda assured her in a voice that didn't sound like her own. She avoided Jace's gaze in the rearview mirror.

How could she tell Marguerite—sweet, gentle Marguerite—that all this anguish was the result of Bea's love for a married man...for her best friend's husband? Amanda might be able to understand her mother, but Jace never would. He'd never loved. He couldn't know how it was to want someone so much that nothing else, no one else, mattered.

The next morning, amid a storm of protest from Marguerite and Amanda, Bea left for Nassau. She and Reese would wait until Amanda was well enough to attend the ceremony, she promised, pushing the date up a month. Reese wouldn't mind, she assured her daughter.

"He's a dear man," she told Amanda. "I think you'll appreciate him even more when you get to know him. You must come and stay with us."

Amanda smiled at the mother she'd only just begun to know. "I may need to," she agreed with a secretive smile.

Bea hugged her tightly. "Are you sure you'll be all right?"

"I'll be fine now. Really, I will."

Bea kissed the pale cheek and went out without looking back—a habit she'd formed early in life—and allowed Marguerite to take her to the airport. Amanda wished silently that she might have been well enough to go with her mother and run away.

But as she found out later, lying in the lovely blue room, staring at the ceiling with a horribly throbbing head, she wasn't in any condition for travel.

The one bright spot in the day was the arrival of a florist with a huge bouquet of carnations, roses, baby's breath and heather, sandwiched in with lily of the valley, irises, mums, daisies—a profusion of color and scent.

"For me?" she choked.

The florist grinned, setting the arrangement on her bedside table. "If your name is Amanda Carson."

"If it wasn't, I'd change it right now," she vowed.

"Hope you enjoy them," he said from the door as he closed it.

She struggled into a sitting position, her narrow strapped green gown sliding off one honey-colored shoulder while she leaned over to put her nose to a small yellow rosebud. Whoever had ordered the flowers knew her taste perfectly; knew how much she loved yellow roses and daisies, because they were dominant in the bouquet.

The door opened again and Duncan strolled in, grinning. Amanda caught him around the neck the minute he came within range and hugged him wildly, through a mist of tears, barely noticing that Jace had followed him and was standing just inside the doorway, scowling.

"Oh, Duncan, you angel, what a wonderful thing to do," she cried, sobbing and laughing all at once as she kissed his lean cheek, oblivious to the puzzled look on his face and the fury in Jace's.

"Huh?" Duncan blinked.

"The flowers, silly." She laughed, and her eyes danced as they had when she was still a girl, lighting up her sad, wan face like a torch so that she was exquisitely beautiful with her silver-blond hair cascading around her, and the thin green gown emphasizing her peaches-and-cream complexion and dark eyes. "They're so beautiful. No one ever sent me flowers before, did you know? And I...what is it?" she asked as he continued to stare vacantly at her.

"I'm glad you like them, but I didn't do it, darling," he admitted sheepishly.

"Then who...?"

Jace turned and left the room before she could continue, and Amanda frowned after him. It couldn't be...could it?

Her fingers trembled as she reached for the card and fumbled the envelope open.

"Must have been Terry...no, it couldn't have been," Duncan corrected, frowning, "because we thought it would save explanations if we didn't bother him. And if Mother had done it, she'd have said something..."

Amanda was reading the card, tears welling suddenly in the eyes she closed on a pain that shuddered all through her body. The card fell lightly to the blue coverlet, like a frail white leaf loosened from its stem by a faint, cold breeze.

There was no message on the white card. Only a black, bold scrawl that was as familiar as her own, and a single four-letter name. "Jace."

Chapter Nine

Jace didn't go near her for the rest of the day, and she knew that she'd hurt him. Despite his scorn for Beatrice Carson, it was clear that he was still vulnerable to her daughter. Had the flowers been a peace offering?

Duncan sat and played gin rummy with her all evening, winning hand after hand until she finally refused to play with him anymore out of sheer exasperation.

"Spoilsport," he goaded. "It's early yet. You're going to force me to go out in search of other entertainment."

"Don't call me names, you cheating cardsharp," she said in her best Western drawl. "I ought to call you out and plug you, stranger."

"The marshal don't like gunplay in this here town," he replied narrow-eyed.

She tossed her hair. "A likely story. You, sir, are simply cowardly."

"Yes, miss, I sho is!" He grinned.

She lay back against the pillows with a weary smile. "Thanks for keeping me company, Duncan. I do feel better now. In fact, I may even be able to get up in the morning."

"Don't push it."

"I have to." She studied her clasped hands. "I have to leave just as soon as I can," she ground out. "I can't take being around Jace much longer."

"He won't bite," he promised her.

She smiled wanly. "Care to bet?"

He drew a deep breath. "Exactly what is going on? Can't you tell me?"

She shook her head. "Private, I'm afraid."

"That sounds ominous, like guns at ten paces or something," he teased, and his brown eyes danced at her.

"I almost wish it was, but he'd have me outgunned on the first draw," she admitted. "I can't fight Jace and win. I don't think anyone can."

"I'm not so sure about that."

"I am."

"Getting sleepy?"

She shook her head. "Just worn out. I didn't even mange to finish my supper, I was so tired."

"You'll be up raiding the kitchen before dawn, mark my words," he scolded.

She laughed. "Maybe."

Duncan's prediction came true shortly after midnight, when she found that she couldn't ignore her growling stomach an instant longer.

She slipped on her old robe and slippers and opened the

door into the hall. She tiptoed past Jace's darkened room, her heart shaking her briefly with its beat, and down the dimly lit stairs. Her feet made no noise at all on the carpet, and she found the kitchen without a slip and turned on the light.

Marguerite's kitchen was absolutely spotless—mosaic tile floors, done in the same blue-and-white motif as the bathrooms, looked recently polished, and the huge stove that Mrs. Brown used for baking was a blazing white. The big counters and huge oak cabinets were a cook's dream. So was the long solid oak table used to prepare food on. There were two or three chairs scattered around, and frilly blue curtains at the darkened windows. Amanda thought idly that it would be a pleasure to work in.

The clean pots and pans cried to be used, so she opened the double-doored refrigerator, knowing her hostess wouldn't mind if she made herself a snack. She pulled out eggs and a big ham, and took down some spices from the cabinet, proceeding quietly to make herself a huge, mouth-watering omelet. She was in the middle of cooking it when the back door suddenly swung open and Jace walked in.

She froze at the sight of him, and he didn't look any less stunned to see her standing at the stove in her robe, her blond hair in a lovely tangle around her shoulders, hanging down to her waist in back.

He was wearing a suede jacket and his familiar black Stetson, jeans that were layered in dust, and old boots with scuffed toes. He didn't look like a corporate executive. He looked the way Jason Whitehall used to look when she was a girl—like a cowboy struggling to carve an empire out of a few hundred head of cattle, a lot of sweat, and a generous amount of business sense.

"What are you doing out of bed?" he asked quietly, closing the door behind him.

"I was hungry," she replied softly.

He glanced toward the pan she was holding on the burner.

"That smells like an omelet," he said.

"It is." She checked it to make sure it wasn't burning. "Ham and egg."

"It smells delicious."

She glanced at him. He looked hungry, too. And cold and tired. There were gray hairs at his temples that she'd barely noticed before, and new lines in his hard face. "Want some?" she asked gently.

"Got enough?" he countered.

She nodded. "I'll make some coffee...."

"I'll make it. Women never get it strong enough." He shrugged out of his jacket to disclose a faded blue-patterned cotton shirt, and threw it onto an empty chair with his hat. He found the coffeepot and proceeded to fill it with apparent expertise while Amanda took up the omelet and put bread into the toaster.

"Butter," she murmured, turning back toward the refrigerator.

"I'll get it," he said.

She took out the toast and laid it on one plate while she went to the cabinet to get a second one for him.

Jace leaned on the counter, but his silvery eyes followed her all around the kitchen, quiet and strange, tracing the slender lines of her body in the old blue terry-cloth robe.

She barely glanced at him as she came back with the plate and set it down on the counter. Her heart was doing acrobatics in her chest, but she tried to look calm, working with deft, efficient hands to divide the omelet, and giving him the lion's share of it.

"Hold it," he said, laying a quick hand on her wrist. "That's more than half."

His touch was warm and light, but she looked down at the lean, darkly tanned fingers with a sense of impending disaster, her face flushing at the emotions playing havoc inside her.

"I…wasn't really that hungry," she admitted. She glanced up at him shyly, and away again. "You…don't look like you even had supper."

He traced a rough pattern on the soft flesh of her wrist. "I didn't."

She moved away from him to put the pan in the sink, wondering at the strange mood he was in.

"Is something wrong?" she asked.

"Only with me," he said on a rough side. "I couldn't sleep."

She stared down at the soapy water in the frying pan. "I'm sorry about the flowers," she whispered. "I didn't realize…that you'd sent them." Her eyes closed. "You've been so cruel."

"Because I told you the truth about your mother?" he demanded. "Why not? You're old enough."

She turned, staring across into his blazing eyes. "Did you have to be so brutal about it?" she asked.

"There's no other way with you," he said quietly. "At least it gets your attention."

Her lips parted. "I don't understand."

He laughed mirthlessly. "Of course not."

Her eyes pleaded with him. "Jace, can't you find it in your heart to forgive her?"

"Forgive her? She's nothing but a slut!" he ground out. "Like her daughter," he added coldly.

She drew in a harsh, hurt breath. "You think you know everything there is to know about me, don't you?"

"All I need to know," he agreed.

"How wonderful to never make a mistake, to never be wrong!" she cast at him.

He turned and caught her blazing eyes with his own. "I make mistakes," he corrected quietly. "I made my biggest one with you."

"How, by not shooting me instead of the bull?" she choked.

"By not taking you into my bed when you were sixteen," he said quietly, and there was no mockery, no teasing light in his eyes now.

Her face went blood red. "As if I'd have gone!" she cried.

"I could have had you the other night," he reminded her, his eyes narrowing. "You were a great deal more vulnerable than that when you were sixteen, and you wanted me even more than you do now."

"That's a lie!" she gasped, outraged.

"The only difference," he continued coldly, "is that it wasn't permissible back then, when the Whitehalls were still just middle class. Now that the shoe's on the other foot, it's perfectly all right for you to want me. Even to give in to me. And why not—it wouldn't be the first time."

Her fingers clenched on the handle on the pan in the sink, and she felt pain as she gripped it.

"I'd rather take poison," she breathed.

One corner of his chiseled mouth went up. "Really?" His eyes swept down over her slender body. "So would I.

You can arouse me when you try, but then, so could anything in skirts. One body's the same as another to a hungry man."

"Go to hell!" she burst out.

"I've been there," he told her. "I don't recommend it. Come and eat your omelet, Amanda, before it gets cold. These coy little performances are beginning to wear on my temper."

He took the plates to the table. Amanda let go of the pan and started blindly toward the dining room, her face stark white, her heart shaking her with its anguished beat. All she wanted from life at that moment was to escape from him.

But he wasn't about to let her escape that easily. He reached out and caught her wrist in a steely grasp, halting her in place.

"You're not going anywhere," he said in a dangerous undertone. "I said sit down."

She licked her dry lips nervously and sat down at the table in the seat he indicated. But she only stared at the omelet through her tears, feeling so sick she was afraid to take a bite of it.

Jace laid down his fork and moved his chair close to hers. "Amanda?"

There was a foreign softness to his deep voice. It was the final undoing. A sob broke from her throat and let the dam of tears overflow down her cheeks until her slender body was shaking helplessly with them.

"For God's sake, don't!" he growled.

"Please…let me go to bed," she pleaded brokenly. "Please…!"

"Oh, hell." He pulled a clean handkerchief from his

pocket and mopped up her tears, and all the anger and spite seemed to go out of him at once. "Here, eat your omelet," he said gently, as if he was speaking to a small child. "Come on. Let me see you taste yours first."

"Why?" she sniffled, looking up at him through tear-spiked lashes.

"I hear that you've been threatening to make me a bowl of buttered toadstools," he mused, and a faint smile eased the rigid lines of his face. "I'd hate to think you laced this omelet with them."

She smiled involuntarily, and her face lit up. He watched the change in her, fascinated.

"I wouldn't poison you," she whispered.

"Wouldn't you, honey?" he asked gently. His fingers reached out to touch, very lightly, the tracks of tears on her flushed cheeks. "Not even with all the provocation I've given you?"

She studied his darkly tanned face solemnly. "I'm sorry," she said.

"For what?"

Her eyes fell to the deep yellow omelet with its cubes of pink ham on her plate. "About what…my mother did."

He drew in a sharp breath. "Eat your omelet."

She stared across at his impassive face as he turned his attention to his own plate.

"Not bad," he murmured after a taste. "When did you learn to cook?"

"When we moved to San Antonio," she said, picking up her fork to speak a chunk of omelet. "I didn't have much choice. Mother couldn't cook at all, and we couldn't afford to eat out." She smiled as she chewed and swallowed the fluffy mouthful. "The first time I tried to fry squash I cut it up raw into the pan and didn't put a drop of oil in it. You could smell it all over the building."

He glanced at her, and one corner of his mouth went up. "You didn't eat that night, I gather."

"Not much." She laughed. "I forgot to salt the macaroni, and burned the meat..." Her voice sighed in memory. "I'm still not a good cook, but I'm better than I was." She studied his rough, arrogant profile. "You learned to cook in the service, didn't you?"

That seemed to surprise him. He stared at her searchingly before he turned his attention to his coffee. "One of my specialties was fried snake," he said dryly.

"Green Berets, wasn't it?" she recalled with a tiny smile as she toyed with her toast. "I remember how striking you used to look in uniform...."

"You were just a baby then," he teased.

"I'm glad," she said suddenly, as a blinding thought floored her. How would it have been all those years ago to have been a woman, and in love with Jace as she was now—to watch the afternoon newscasts knowing he and his unit were so far away and fighting for their lives....

"What's the matter?" he asked quietly.

She shook her head. "Nothing."

He swallowed down his coffee and leaned back in his chair. "Where do you live in San Antonio?" he asked conversationally.

She glanced at him and away. It was as if Bea had never come. They were talking now as they had that day at the restaurant—freely, openly, like two people who understood and respected one another.

"In a one-bedroom efficiency apartment," she replied.

"Right downtown. I can walk to work, and it's convenient to the corner grocery store, too."

"You don't own a car?"

"Can't afford one," she said sheepishly. Her soft brown eyes teased his. "They break down."

He drew a long, slow breath. His lean hand went up to unfasten the top buttons on his shirt, as if the warmth of the kitchen was uncomfortable for him. Her eyes involuntarily followed the movement and he smiled sensuously at her.

"Want me to take it off?" he asked in a lazy, teasing drawl.

She caught her breath, remembering without wanting to the feel of that mat of thick, curling hair on his chest under her fingers.

She averted her eyes, wrapping both hands around her coffee cup.

He chuckled softly, but he didn't stop until he'd opened the shirt all the way down, baring his bronzed chest in the sudden tense stillness of the room. His hand rubbed over it roughly and he drew in a long, heavy yawn.

"God, I'm so tired," he said heavily.

"Why did you send the flowers?" she asked. An instant later she could have bitten her tongue for the impulsive question.

His silver eyes searched hers. "You might have died," he said bluntly, "and I'd have been responsible. The flowers were by way of apology," he added gruffly, looking away. "I never meant you to be hurt like that."

She stared at his sharp profile, knowing how it shook that towering pride of his to admit he was sorry about anything. And suddenly she realized how much it must have hurt him to know that his father was unfaithful to Marguerite. Knowing it, trying to protect his mother.... All her own pain fell away as she studied him, just beginning to understand his point of view.

"Would you listen, if I explained something to you?" she asked gently.

His silver eyes cut at her. "Not if it's about your mother," he said bluntly.

She drew in a sharp breath, her cold hands clenching around the coffee cup. "Jason, have you ever been in love?" she asked harshly. "So deeply in love that nothing and no one else mattered? I don't pretend to know how your father felt, but Mother loved him beyond anything on earth. There was never anyone but Jude for her, not even my own father. It was a once-in-a-lifetime kind of love, and she had the bad luck to feel it for a married man. I'm not condoning what she did, but I can at least understand why she did it. She loved him, Jace."

His eyes dropped to the table. "When is the wedding?" he asked curtly.

"In a month. I'll be joining Mother and Reese in the Bahamas for the ceremony."

He studied her downbent head. "And in the meantime?"

"I'm going back to San Antonio as soon as I'm well enough to travel," she said honestly, tears in her voice. "You can let Terry know your decision about the account," she added in a whisper.

He drew in a weary breath. "As far as I'm concerned, it's yours. You can iron out the details with Duncan." He stood up. "If you want to leave here that badly, go ahead."

Her lovely eyes filled with tears as she looked up at him. He wasn't going to bend an inch. He could let her walk away, out of his life, and not feel a thing. But she loved him too much to let go.

"Is that what you want?" she asked bravely, her face pale in the soft light of the kitchen.

His jaw tautened, his silver eyes narrowed. "You know what I want."

Yes, she knew all too well. Perhaps Bea was right. Love was the most important thing. A few hours in Jace's arms might not be proper, but it would be a soft memory to wrap around herself in the long, empty years ahead. She loved him so much. Would it be so wrong to spend just one night with him?

"All right," she said softly, her tone weak but unfaltering.

He scowled down at her. "All right, what?" he asked.

She lifted her face proudly. "I'll sleep with you."

His nostrils flared with a sharp indrawn breath. "In return for what, exactly?" he asked harshly.

"Does everything have to have a price tag?" she murmured miserably, standing up. "I want nothing from you!"

"Amanda!"

She stopped at the doorway, her back to him. "Yes?"

There was a brief, poignant silence. "If you want me, come back here and prove it."

She almost ran. It would have been in character, and it was what she would have done a few months earlier. But now she knew there was more to Jason's ardor than an angry kiss in the moonlight. She knew how exquisitely tender he could be, how patient. And her need of him was too great to ignore. There was no limit to the demands he could make on her now that she knew how desperately she loved him.

She turned and went back to him, pausing at the table, her eyes faintly apprehensive as they looked up into his. He hadn't moved at all, and his gaze was calculating as it met hers.

"Well?" he asked.

She moved closer, searching her mind for a few clues as to what would be expected of her. She'd never tried to seduce a man before. A couple of old movies came to mind, but one called for her to crawl into his sleeping bag and the other would only work if she could already be undressed and in his bed when he came out of the shower.

Experimentally, she linked her hands around his neck and reached up on tiptoe to brush her lips against his jutting chin. He wouldn't bend an inch to help her, and his chin was as far as she could reach.

"You might help me a little," she pointed out, puzzled by the faint amusement in his silver eyes.

"What do you want me to do?" he asked obligingly.

"If you'd bend your head just an inch or so...."

He bent down, watching her as she looked up at him hesitantly. Nervous, inhibited, it was all she could do to make that first movement toward him, to put her mouth against his and yield her body to the strength of his.

She closed her eyes and pressed herself against his tall frame, her mouth suddenly hungry as the love she felt melted into her veins like a drug. But it wasn't enough. It was like kissing stone, and even when she increased the pressure of her lips, he didn't seem to feel the need to respond.

She drew away and looked up at him, her eyes soft with hunger, her breath unsteady. "Oh, Jace, teach me how..." she whispered brokenly.

His eyes widened, only to narrow and glitter down at her, something passing across his face like a faint shadow as his hands touched her waist and untied the robe with a lazy, deft twist.

She caught his hands as he eased the robe down her arms, leaving her standing before him in only the pale mint gown that was all but transparent, its low neckline giving more than a glimpse of her small, perfect breasts.

"You offered something to me," he reminded her, something calculating in his gaze. "Cold feet, Amanda?"

She swallowed nervously. "No," she lied. She let him dispose of the robe, looping it over the chair she'd vacated. His fingers went to the thin spaghetti straps that held the bodice of the gown in place, toying with the bow ties.

"Jason, it's getting late!" she whispered, feeling a sense of panic, the age-old fear of a woman with her first man.

"Easy, honey," he murmured, his hands suddenly soothing on her back, his lips gentle as they touched her flushed face. "Just relax, Amanda, I know what I'm doing. Relax, honey, I'm not going to rush you, all right? That's better," he mused, feeling some of the tension ease out of her with the leisure of his movements, his tone. "Are you afraid of making love with me?" he whispered.

She swallowed down her fear. "Of course not," she managed in a voice straight from the tomb.

"Show me."

She drew back and looked up at him helplessly; it was like being told to play an instrument when she'd never learned to read music. Her look pleaded with him.

His eyes narrowed, but not in anger. Some strange, quiet glow made them darken. He looked down at her with a kind of triumph as one deft hand flicked open the bow on her shoulder. He repeated the gesture with the other bow and held her eyes while the gauzy fabric slid unimpeded to her waist and she felt the soft breeze from the open window on her sudden bareness.

She blushed like a schoolgirl, hating her own inexperience, hating the expertise behind his action, frightened at the intimacy between them even though she'd initiated it.

His eyes dropped to the high, soft curves he'd uncovered, studying them in the tense silence that followed.

"My God, you're lovely," he said quietly. "As sweet as a prayer…."

She caught her breath. "What…an incredible way to put it," she whispered.

He drew his eyes back up to hers. "What did you expect, Amanda, some vulgar remark? What's happening between us isn't cheap, and you're not a woman I picked up on the street. You belong to me, every soft inch of you, and there's nothing shameful about my looking at you. You're exquisite."

Her eyes held his, reading the tenderness in them. "I…like looking at you, too," she said breathlessly, her fingers lightly touching the powerful contours of his chest, tangling gently in the wiry, curling dark hair over the warm bronzed muscles.

"Mandy…" he breathed, drawing her very gently to him until her softness melted into his hardness, until she could feel the hair-roughened muscles pressing against her own taut breasts, and he heard her gasp.

"Now kiss me," he whispered huskily, bending his head, "and let me show you how much we can say to each other without words."

He took her mouth with a controlled ferocity that made her breath catch in her throat, tasting it, savoring it, in a silence wild with the newness of discovery. She lifted her arms around neck, holding him, her body trembling where its bareness was crushed warmly to his until she felt such a part of him that nothing short of death could separate them. She loved him so! To be in his arms, to feel the raw hunger of his mouth cherishing hers, penetrating it, devouring it, was as close to paradise as she'd ever been. Tears welled in her eyes at the intensity of what she was feeling with him, at the depth of the love she couldn't deny even when she cursed it for making her weak.

His arms contracted at her back and ground her body into his for an instant before he lifted his head and looked down into her soft, yielding eyes.

"I want one word from you," he said in a gruff, unsteady voice, and the arms that held her had a fine tremor. "I ache like a boy with his first woman, and I can't take much more of this."

She knew exactly what he meant, and there was only one way she could answer him after the way she'd responded. She loved him more than her own life, and even though she'd probably hate both of them in daylight, the soft darkness and the sweet pleasure of his body against hers would be a memory she could hold for the long, empty years ahead without him.

She opened her mouth to speak, to tell him, when the beautiful dream they were sharing was shattered by the sudden, loud roar of a car's engine coming up the driveway.

Jace said something violent under his breath and held Amanda close in his arms, burying his face in her throat in a silence bitter with denial until the tremor went out of his arms, until his shuddering heartbeat calmed.

Her fingers soothed him, brushing softly at the cool strands of hair at his temples. "I'm sorry," she whispered tenderly. "I'm sorry."

His lips brushed her silky skin just below her ear and moved up to touch her earlobe. "Are you really?" he whispered. "Or is it like a reprieve?"

"I don't understand," she murmured.

He drew back, his eyes missing nothing as they probed hers. "You're a virgin, aren't you, Amanda," he said quietly.

She flushed, her face giving her away, and he nodded, dropping his eyes to the soft curves pressed so closely against him. "I should have known," he mused, and a corner of his mouth went up as he carefully eased her bodice back in place and lifted her hand to hold it there while he retied the spaghetti straps with a sophisticated carelessness that had her gaping at him.

"I…I tried to tell you before," she faltered, "but you wouldn't listen."

"I was jealous as hell, and hurting," he said bluntly. "Jealous of Black and jealous of my own brother. I thought you came because of Duncan and I wanted to strangle you both."

"You're the only one I wanted," she breathed, her eyes telling all her secrets to him in the soft, sweet silence that followed.

He caught her narrow hips and drew them against the taut, powerful lines of his legs, watching the faint tremor that shook her.

"I like to watch your face when I hold you like this," he said tightly. "Your eyes turn gold when you're aroused."

Her eyes closed on a wave of pure hunger. "Jace," she whispered achingly, clinging to him.

"I want you, too," he whispered back, but for all the wild, fervent hunger she could sense in him, the lips he pressed against her forehead were breathlessly gentle. "Damn Duncan…!" he ground out as the sound of a car door slamming burst onto the silence.

Jace let her go with a rough sigh, his eyes caressing as they swept down her slender body. "You'd better go on up. I'm not in the mood for any of Duncan's witty remarks, and I'd hate to end the day by knocking out any more of his teeth."

She smiled at him, the radiance of her face giving her a soft beauty that made him catch his breath. "Poor Duncan," she murmured.

"Poor Duncan, hell!" He grabbed up her robe and helped her into it, jerking the ties together to pull her body against him. He bent and kissed her roughly, his lips hard, faintly hurting. "You're mine, honey," he told her, his breath warming her mouth. "And I'm not sharing you. Once I take you into my bed, I'll kill another man for touching you."

"Jace!" she whispered, stunned at the cool violence of the words.

"I've waited seven years for you," he said harshly. "I'm through waiting. By the time this weekend is over, you'll belong to me completely."

She stared up at him helplessly, understanding him with a painful clarity. "I…I was going back to San Antonio after the party tomorrow night."

"Was is right," he said, his eyes hard. "You're staying now. I want the whole damned world to know you're mine. There'll be no hushed-up weekends at your apartment, no climbing the back stairs to your bedroom. It's all going to be open and aboveboard, so you'd better start making plans." He released her and turned her around with a slight push in the direction of the door. "Go to bed. We'll talk about it tomorrow night."

She looked over her shoulder at him when she reached the door. "Does…everyone have to know?" she asked, feeling the shame wash over her like the night air.

"Why in hell not?" he wanted to know.

It was different for men. Why should he care? She turned and walked toward the door.

"Amanda!" He studied her face as she turned. "The light's gone out of you. What is it? Something I said?"

"I'm just tired," she assured him with a wan smile. "Just tired, Jason. Good night."

Chapter Ten

Amanda wore a white-and-yellow eyelet sundress downstairs the next morning, her eyes dark-shadowed from lack of sleep, her heart tumbling around wildly in her chest as she approached the dining room. All night she'd agonized over it, and she was no closer to a solution. How did Jace expect her to survive the contempt in his mother's eyes, in Duncan's eyes, when he calmly announced that Amanda was his new mistress? But she loved him so much that the thought of going away, of living without him, was worse than the certainty of death. She cared too much to go now. It would be like leaving half of her soul behind, and she was too weak to bear the separation.

She moved into the carpeted room hesitantly, her eyes colliding instantly with Jace's across the length of the table with the impact of steel against rock. He studied her quietly, one corner of his mouth lifting, his expression impossible to read.

"Good morning, dear," Marguerite said with a smile. "I'm glad you're up early. We've got so much to do to get ready for the party tonight. Now, about your dress..."

"Leave that to me," Jace said with a smile. "I'll take care of it."

Marguerite raised an eyebrow and looked from his smug face to Amanda's flushed one, and smiled. "Anything you say, dear," she murmured, lowering her eyes to her filled plate.

Duncan came in yawning, oblivious to the undercurrents around him. "Good morning." He plopped down in a chair and glanced from Jace to Amanda and grinned. "Everybody sleep well?" he asked.

Amanda's face went redder, and Jace leaned on his forearms, one eye dangerously narrowed as he glared at his brother. He didn't say a word, but he didn't have to. The look had always been adequate.

Duncan grimaced, reaching for cream and sugar to put into his coffee. "Talk about looks that kill...! Have a heart, Jace. I didn't mean a thing."

Marguerite frowned. "Did I miss something?"

"I think we both did," Duncan muttered, irrepressible. "Jace was in the kitchen alone when I got in at two o'clock this morning, looking like a wounded bear."

"Jason always looks like a wounded bear at two o'clock in the morning," his mother reminded him.

"His lip was swollen," Duncan added with a sly glance at Amanda, who swallowed her coffee too fast and choked.

"That doesn't prove anything," Jace said with a half-amused expression.

Amanda, remembering the feel of his lower lip as she nibbled at it, glanced at him and felt the floor reeling out from under her at the shared memory reflected in his silvery eyes.

"Do behave," Marguerite cautioned Duncan. "And where were you until two in the morning, by the way?"

"Following my big brother's sterling example," he replied with a grin at Jace.

"You were at the office working?" Marguerite blinked.

Duncan sighed. "Jace doesn't work all the time."

Marguerite finished her breakfast and drew up her linen napkin with a flourish to dab at her lips. "Duncan, you're in a very strange mood this morning. Perhaps you need a vacation?"

"That's just what I need," Duncan agreed quickly. "How about Hawaii? You could come with me, Mother. The sea air would do you good."

"The sea air gives me infected sinuses," she reminded him. "Besides how could you pick up girls with your mother along? Be sensible."

Duncan laughed. "Oh, Mother, I wouldn't trade you for all Jace's cattle."

Marguerite beamed. "Well, I'd better get busy. Jace..." She studied him a little apprehensively. "You will be kind to Amanda?"

He lowered his eyes to his coffee cup. "I'll make an effort," he assured her.

"Good. Duncan, would you drive me? My car's acting up, I'm going to have the garage take it in for inspection," she fired at her youngest son, as she started out the door.

"But, I'm still eating..." Duncan protested, a forkful of egg halfway to his mouth.

"Finish it when we get back," she returned implacably.

Duncan stared at the egg and put it down. "I'll buy myself a stale doughnut or something," he murmured wistfully. "Bye, all," he called over his shoulder, winking at Amanda.

Once they were out of the room, Jace looked up, his eyes catching Amanda's, holding them.

"Hello," he said softly.

Wild thrills ran through her at the lazy tone, the smile. "Hello," she whispered back, her eyes lighting up like soft brown lights, her face radiant.

"I like you in white and yellow," he remarked, studying her. "You remind me of a daisy."

"Daisies don't tell," she remarked, clutching her coffee cup to still the trembling of her hands.

He smiled, drawing her eyes to the chiseled mouth her own had clung to so hungrily the night before. His lower lip was just slightly swollen.

"Duncan doesn't miss a trick," he remarked with a deep chuckle.

She flushed delightfully. "I'm sorry," she said gently.

"Why? I like those sharp little teeth," he murmured sensuously. "I could feel them nibbling at my mouth long after I showered and went to bed."

She didn't even feel the heat of the cup in her hand. "I thought I'd never sleep...."

"That makes two of us," he agreed. His face was expressionless, suddenly, his eyes blazing the length of the table at her. "Come here."

She put the cup down and went to him, dazed at the newness of being able to look at him without fear of discovery, without having to explain it. He caught her around the waist and pulled her down onto his lap, letting her head fall back against his shoulder so that he could look down at her. He smelled of expensive cologne, and his soft brown silk shirt was smooth against her cheek, his tanned throat visible at the open neck.

"I almost came for you last night," he said quietly, his eyes dark and faintly smiling. "That damned bed was so big and empty, and I wanted you almost beyond bearing."

"I didn't sleep, either," she admitted. Her fingers reached up to trace his mouth. She noted that he was clean-shaven now, the smoothness of his skin a contrast to the faint raspiness which had been there last night.

He tipped her mouth up and bent to kiss her. His lips were slow, tender, easing hers apart to deepen the kiss, his breath coming quicker as he grasped the nape of her neck and suddenly crushed her mouth under his in a hungry, deep passion. The kiss seemed to go on forever, slow and hard and faintly bruising in the soft silence of the dining room. His arms brought her up closer, cradling her, the sounds of silk rustling against cotton invading her ears along with her own faint moan as she returned the kiss with her whole heart.

Her fingers went to the buttons on his shirt and she unbuttoned it slowly, only half aware of what she was doing, consumed with the need to touch him, to savor the sensuous maleness of his hair-roughened flesh.

He caught her hand as it tangled in the curling hair, drawing back a little, his eyes narrow, his heart pounding heavily in his chest. "If you touch me, I'm going to touch you," he said gruffly. "And we don't have time for what it would lead to."

She licked her dry lips, aware of the warm pressure of his lean fingers where they pressed hers to his body. "Would it lead to that?" she whispered.

"The way I feel right now, yes," he replied. His mouth

brushed her closed eyelids. "Oh, God, I love for you to touch me," he whispered huskily.

She smiled, leaning her flushed cheek against his chest. "It's so strange…."

"What is?" he murmured against her forehead.

"Not fighting you."

He drew a long, slow breath. "I've given you hell for a long time."

"Maybe you had reason to." She sighed softly. "Jace, I'm sorry about Mother…."

He touched his forefinger against her lips, looking down at her with a strange, brooding expression. "I'm not over it, yet," he said quietly. "But I think I'm beginning to understand. Emotions aren't always so easy to control. God knows, I lose my head every time I touch you."

She smiled lazily. "Is that so bad?"

"For me it is. I've never been demonstrative. I've had women, but always on my terms, and never one I couldn't walk away from." He looked down at her, scowling. "You make me feel sensations I didn't know I could experience. They wash over my body like fire when I hold you, when I touch you…you pleasure me, Amanda. That's an old-fashioned phrase, but I can't think of anything more descriptive."

She drew her hand against his hard cheek. "I think we pleasure each other," she said quietly. "Do I really belong to you?"

"Do you want to?"

She nodded, unashamed, her eyes worshiping every line of his face.

He drew his hand across her waist, trailing it up over the fabric across her firm, high breasts, pausing to cup one of them warmly, his eyes darting to catch the stunned expression on her face.

"You'll get used to being touched like this," he said softly.

"Will I?" she managed breathlessly.

His eyes searched hers. "I hadn't thought about it until now, but you've never let a man look at you the way I did last night, have you? I'd always thought you were experienced until I saw that wild blush on your face. And when I held you like that..." He smiled gently. "I'll remember it the rest of my life. More than anything, I wanted to be the one to teach you about love. I thought you'd given that privilege to some other man, and I hated you for it."

"I never wanted anyone but you," she said simply, her eyes sad as she thought how little of him she'd really have when it was all over. He'd tire of her innocence eventually, he'd tire of being with her. They had so much in common, but all he wanted was her body, not her mind or her heart.

"What's wrong?" he asked softly.

She shrugged. "Nothing. What did you mean about a dress?"

"Curious?" He chuckled, putting her back on her feet. "Come on and I'll show you."

He led her into the exclusive department store, straight to the women's department, to the couture section. She pulled back, but he wouldn't let go of her hand. He turned her over to the sleek saleslady with a description of the kind of dress he wanted her to try on for him.

"Yes, sir, Mr. Whitehall," the poised, middle-aged woman said with a smile. "I have just the thing...!"

"But I don't want you to buy me a dress," Amanda protested as the saleslady sailed away toward the back.

Jace only smiled, his eyes hooded, mysterious. "Why not? Did you plan to go to the party in slacks?"

That hurt. It hadn't mattered so much, being without, until he made such a point of it. And to have the people in this exclusive store know that he was buying her clothes—what were they going to think? She might as well be some man's bought woman. Her eyes misted. Well, it was the truth, wasn't it? She'd already promised herself to him.

Her eyes lowered, her face paper-white.

"What is it?" he asked gently, lifting her face to his puzzled eyes. "Honey, what did I say?"

She tried to smile and shook her head, but she was choking to death on her pride.

"Here it is," the saleslady cooed, reappearing with a fantasy of hand-painted organza which she was holding up carefully by the hanger. It was sheer and off-white with a delicate pattern of tiny green leaves. The bodice was held in place by swaths of the same silky fabric. Amanda, even when she'd had money to burn, had never seen anything so lovely.

"Just perfect," the saleslady promised, and named the house it had been designed by. Before Amanda could protest, she was shuttled off to a fitting room, where she was eased into the dream of luxury by deft, cool hands.

She stared at herself in the mirror. It had been so long since she'd worn such an expensive dress, felt the richness of organza against her slender body. The pale green highlighted her deep brown eyes, lent a hint of mystery to the shadows of her face. The color was good for her honey tan skin, too, giving it a rich gold color that went well with her long, wispy curls of silvery blond hair.

"Are you going to spend the day in there?" a deep, impatient voice grumbled from just outside the curtain.

She shifted her shoulders and walked out gracefully, her eyes apprehensive as his lightning gaze whipped over her while the saleslady stood smugly to one side.

"Isn't it just perfect?" the older woman said with a smile.

"Perfect," Jace said quietly, but he was looking at Amanda's flushed face, not at the dress, and the look in his silver eyes made her knees go weak. "I'll take it."

Amanda took the dress off and waited for it to be boxed, her eyes on Jace's expressionless face.

"I haven't asked the price," she said softly, "but it's going to be an arm and a leg, Jace. I'd really rather get something…less costly."

"I'm not poor," he reminded her with a wry glance. "Remember?"

Her eyes lowered. She felt faintly sick inside. Was that what he thought of her, that she'd finally given in for mercenary reasons, that she was allowing herself to be bought for a few pretty clothes and an unlimited allowance? She stood with her head bowed while Jace got out his credit card and took care of the details. He handed her the box with the exclusive store name on it, watching quietly as she stared down at it blankly.

He sighed heavily, turning away. "Let's go," he said tightly.

He unlocked the door of his silver Mercedes and, taking the box from her, tossed it carelessly into the back seat before he went around and got in behind the wheel. There was a carefully controlled violence in the way he started the car and pulled it out into traffic.

"Well, don't you like the damned dress?" he asked shortly.

"It's very nice. Thank you."

"Will you please, damn it, tell me what's upset you?" he asked, slanting an irritated glance at her.

"Nothing," she said softly. Her eyes were staring straight ahead, her heart breaking.

"Nothing." His hands tightened on the wheel. "This isn't the best way to begin a relationship, doe-eyes."

"I know." She drew in a steadying breath. "I love the dress, Jason. I just…I wish you hadn't spent so much on me."

"Don't you think you're worth it, honey? I do." He reached across the console and took her hand in his, locking his hard, cool fingers into hers with a slow, sensuous pressure that made her breath catch.

She stared down at his brown fingers, so dark against her soft tan. His hand squeezed warmly, swallowing hers, his thumb caressing. "You're so dark," she murmured.

"And you're so fair," he replied. He glanced at her briefly before he turned his attention back to traffic. "I'm sorry I have to go to the office. I'd rather spend the day with you."

She sighed wistfully, looking down again. "I'd have liked that," she murmured absently.

"So would I." He drew his hand away to make a turn, and there was a comfortable silence between them until they pulled up in front of the house. "I won't be here until the last minute, but wait for me," he told her. "You're going to the Sullevans' with me, not with Duncan."

"Yes, Jason," she said gently.

He leaned across her to open the door, his face barely an inch away, and she could smell the expensive tang of his cologne, the smoky warmth of his breath. Her eyes lingered on the hard lines of his dark face and involuntarily fell to his mouth. Impulsively she moved her head a fraction of an inch and brushed her lips against his.

He caught his breath, his eyes suddenly fiery, burning with emotion.

"Sorry," she whispered, shaken by the violence in the look.

"For what?" he asked tautly. "Do you have to have permission to kiss me, to touch me?"

"I…I'm not used to it."

"I told you this morning," he said gruffly, "I love the feel of your hands on me. My God, you could climb into bed with me if you felt like it, and I'd hold my arms open for you, don't you know that?"

She reached up and tentatively brushed a strand of hair away from his broad forehead, her eyes warm on his face. "It's so new," she whispered.

"Yes." He bent and took her mouth gently under his, probing her soft lips, his breath whispering against her cheek as his hand held her throat, holding her face up. "Oh, God, your mouth is so soft," he whispered tenderly, "I could spend the rest of my life kissing you."

She reached up and slid her arms around his neck. "I like kissing you, too," she murmured. She kissed him back, hard, her arms possessive.

"Don't go to work," she whispered.

"If I stay here, I'll make love to you," he murmured against her eager mouth, his hands cupping her face while he tasted every sweet curve of her lips. "And I don't want to do that yet."

"I think that's a terrible thing to say," she murmured back.

His lips smiled against hers. "I want it to be just right with you," he whispered.

She felt a tingle of excitement run the length of her body as the words made pictures in her mind. Jace's body against hers on cool, crisp sheets, the darkness all around them, his mouth on her soft skin...

"You trembled," he whispered softly. "Thinking about how it would be with me?"

"Yes," she admitted breathlessly.

"God...!" He half lifted her across the seat, crushing her against his hard chest, his mouth suddenly rough, demanding, as it opened on hers. She went under in a maze of surging emotion, moaning softly at the hunger he was arousing.

All at once he let her go, easing her away from him breath by breath, his eyes stormy, hungry. "Get out of here before I wrestle you down on the floorboard," he murmured half-humorously.

"Pagan," she breathed, easing her long legs out the door.

"Puritan," he countered. "I'll see you tonight. And don't put your hair up. Leave it like that."

She got her box out and stared at him through the open door. "It won't look elegant enough," she argued.

"I don't want you elegant," he returned, his eyes sliding over her. "I want you just the way you are, no changes. Remember, wait for me."

"All right."

He closed the door and drove off without looking back.

That evening she stood in her bedroom, dressed in the exquisite gown Jace had bought for her. It fit like a caressing glove. She stared in the mirror as if she'd never seen her own reflection, marvelling at the soft lines that emphasized all her best features. With its curling mass of layered ruffles the frothy skirt drew attention to her long, slender legs. The bodice clung to her small, high breasts, draping across them with just a hint of sensuality. And the cut emphasized just how tiny her waist really was. The green-and-white pattern was the perfect foil for her blond fairness, lending her a sophistication far beyond her years. With her hair long and soft down her back, she looked more like a model than an advertising executive.

She was nervous when she went downstairs an hour later, to join Jace and Duncan and Marguerite in the living room where they were enjoying a last-minute drink.

They were deep in a discussion, but Jace turned in time to watch her entrance, and something flashed like silver candles in his eyes as they traveled slowly over her. Something strangely new lingered there...pride...possession...

Her own eyes were drawn to the figure he cut in his elegant evening clothes. The darkness of the suit, added to the frothy whiteness of his silk shirt, gave him a suave masculinity that made her want to touch him. He was devastating, like something out of a men's fashion magazine, and as completely unaware of his own attraction as a cat of its mysterious eyes.

Two other heads turned abruptly, their attention caught by the utter silence, and Duncan let loose a long, leering whistle.

"Wow!" he burst out, moving forward to walk around her like a prospective buyer around a sleek new car. "If you aren't a dream and a half. Where did you get that dress?"

"The tooth fairy brought it," she said lightly, avoiding Jace's possessive eyes.

Marguerite laughed. "You're a vision, Amanda. What a lovely dress!"

"Thank you," she murmured demurely.

Duncan started to take her arm, only to find Jace there ahead of him. "My turn, I think," he said with a level look that started Duncan backstepping.

"Who am I to argue?" Duncan teased. He turned to Marguerite. "Mother?"

Marguerite moved forward, very elegant in her pale blue satin gown and fox stole. "Oh, Amanda, I forgot... your arms will chill in the night air!"

"No, they won't!" Amanda argued quickly, already dreading that chill, but too proud to accept charity.

"Nonsense! I have a lovely shawl. Just a minute." And she walked to the hall closet, coming instantly back with a black mantilla-style shawl which she draped around the young girl's shoulders. "Now! Just the thing, too. It makes you look mysterious."

"I feel rather mysterious," Amanda said with a smile, and caught her breath as Jace came up beside her to guide her out the door with a lean, warm hand at her waist.

Amanda had never been as aware of Jace as she was on the way to the Sullevans' house. Her eyes were involuntarily drawn to his hard profile, his mouth, and she felt swirls of excitement running over her smooth skin at the memory of his kisses. He glanced sideways once and met her searching eyes as they stopped for a red light, and the force of his gaze knocked the breath out of her. She let her eyes fall to his lean, strong hands on the steering wheel, and it was all she could do not to lean across and run her fingers over them. If only things had been different. She was Jace's woman now, but not the way she wanted to be. He thought she was only interested in his money, when all she truly wanted was to be allowed to love him. Her eyes stared blankly out the window. She wondered miserably how he was going to arrange it all. Would she have an apartment in town? Or would he buy her a house? She flushed, thinking of Marguerite's face when Jace told her. No back alleys, he'd said, but then he wasn't considering how much it was going to hurt Amanda. Why should he, she thought bitterly, he was a man. Men considered their own pleasure, nothing else, and it wouldn't hurt his reputation.

The big house was ablaze with light when they got there, and Amanda felt dwarfed by Jace even in her spiked heels as they walked into the foyer to be met by Mr. Sullevan, Marguerite's co-host. The elegant entranceway was graced by a huge Waterford crystal chandelier, cloud-soft eggshell-white carpet under their feet and priceless objets d'art on dainty tables lining the walls.

"What a showplace!" Duncan murmured, walking into the crowded ballroom with Jace and Amanda while his mother remained behind to help greet the other guests.

"Old money," Jace replied coolly. "This spread was part of a Spanish land grant."

"Well, it's something. And speaking of things that are easy on the eyes," Duncan added with a mock leer at Amanda, "that's an enticing little number you're wearing tonight. You never did tell me where you got it."

Jace's eyes glittered a warning at his brother, and his hand found Amanda's at the same time, linking his fingers with hers in a possessive grasp.

"I bought it for her," he told Duncan, his voice soft and dangerous.

That note in Jace's deep tones was enough for Duncan. He'd heard it too many times not to recognize it.

"Excuse me," he murmured with a wry smile at Amanda. "I think I'll go scout the territory for single beauties. See you later."

Amanda's face was a wild rose. She couldn't even look at Jace. "Was that necessary?" she said in an embarrassed, strangled tone.

"You're mine," he replied curtly. "The sooner he knows it, the safer he's going to be."

She looked up at him. "You made me sound cheap, Jason," she said in a voice that trembled with hurt.

His eyes narrowed, his face hardened at the remark, as if he couldn't believe what she'd said. "What the hell are you talking about? I can't understand you, Amanda. I've already offered you everything I mean to. Now you'd better damn well make up your mind to take it or leave it!"

With a small cry, she tore away from him and ran through the crowd to where Duncan was sipping punch at the buffet table beside the crystal punch bowl.

He took one look at her white face and handed her a small crystal cup of punch, his eyes glancing across the room to Jace's rigid back in a semicircle of local cattlemen.

"You're safe," he told Amanda. "He'll do nothing but talk cattle futures for the next half hour or so. What happened this time?"

Her lower lip trembled. "He said…oh, never mind, Duncan." She sighed wearily. "What's the use? As far as Jason's concerned, the only asset he's got is a fat wallet."

She laughed mirthlessly. "I think I'll become a professional gold digger."

"You haven't got the look," Duncan said blandly. "Have a sandwich."

She took it. "Do I look hungry?" she asked.

"As if you'd like to bite something," he mused, winking. "Don't let him get to you, Mandy. He just doesn't know what's hit him, that's all."

"I wish it were that simple." She sighed with a smile.

"It's not?"

If you only knew, she thought humorously. She stared at the cup of punch and realized she was feeling lightheaded. "What's in this?" she asked.

"Half the liquor cabinet," Duncan replied with a grin. "Go slow."

"Maybe I feel reckless," she replied, throwing down the rest of the punch. She handed him her empty cup. "Pour me another round, masked stranger."

"I don't think this is a wise idea," he reminded her, but he filled the small crystal cup again.

"I don't think so either," she agreed. "It's better not to think—it gets you in trouble."

He watched her quietly. "Know something?" he asked gently.

She peeked up at him over the rim of the cup. "What?"

He smiled. "I'm going to like having you for a sister-in-law."

The tears came unbidden and started rolling down her cheeks. It was the last straw. Duncan, dear Duncan, didn't understand. Jason didn't want a wife—he wanted a mistress, someone to satisfy his passions but not to share his life. And if he ever did marry, it wouldn't be Amanda.

"Mandy!" Duncan burst out, aghast at her reaction.

"What relation will you be to his mistress, Duncan?" she whispered brokenly. "Because that's all he wants me for!"

She turned and ran out onto the dark patio, leaning over the balustrade while she wept like a child.

Duncan stared after her, only dimly aware that someone was standing beside him.

"What the hell did you say to her?" Jace demanded, his eyes blazing.

Duncan blinked at him. "Too much, I'm afraid," he said quietly. His eyes searched his brother's. "I told her I was going to enjoy being her brother-in-law. I guess I jumped the gun, but the way you two have been looking at each other lately, it was a natural assumption."

The older man's face hardened. "You've got a big mouth," he said curtly.

"Amen," Duncan said miserably. He frowned. "Are you serious about her being your mistress?" he asked suddenly, his gaze hard.

Jace's eyes flashed wildly. "Mistress?" he burst out.

"That's what she thinks you want," was the cool reply. "She said you think she's a gold digger."

Jace's eyes closed on a harsh sigh. "Oh, my God."

"What is it?" Duncan asked curiously.

"History repeating itself," Jace ground out. But he wasn't looking at Duncan. His eyes were on the patio through the open doors. He started toward it without another word.

Amanda brushed at the hot tears, her heart weighing her down. She wanted nothing more than to get on a plane and fly away from Casa Verde forever. She needed her head examined for having agreed to stay until tonight. If only she had been well enough to leave with Bea. Then at least she would have been out of Jace's way, out of reach of his sarcasm, his contempt. She never should have offered herself to him. The gift of love she'd thought to make him had only lessened his opinion of her. The tears rushed down her cheeks once more. She'd have to stop this. She'd have to stop crying. Somehow she was going to walk back into that party and smile and pretend she was the belle of the ball, and then she was going to get Duncan to take her to the airport....

"It's quiet out here."

She stiffened at the slow, deep voice behind her. Her hands gripped the stone balustrade, but she didn't turn.

"Yes," she murmured coldly.

She felt rather than heard him move behind her. She could feel the warmth of his body against her back, feel his breath in her hair.

His fingers lightly touched the wispy curls over her shoulders and she tensed involuntarily.

"Amanda..." he began heavily.

"I'm going home," she said without preamble, brushing away the rest of the tears with the back of her hands. "And you can have the dress back, I don't want it. Give it to one of your other women," she added curtly.

"There hasn't been another woman," he replied, his voice clipped, measured. "Not since you were sixteen years old and I felt your mouth under mine for the first time."

She froze against the cold stone. Had she heard him right? Surely her ears were playing tricks on her! She turned around slowly, and looked up into his shadowed eyes. Their silver glitter was just faintly visible in the light from the noisy ballroom.

He rammed his hands into his pockets and glared down at her, his legs apart, his body tall and faintly arrogant in the stance. "Shocked?" he asked shortly. "Are you too innocent to realize that the reason I was so hungry for you was that I hadn't had a woman in years?"

"Not…for lack of opportunity, surely," she managed unsteadily.

"I've had that," he agreed, nodding. "I'm rich. Women, most of them, would do anything for money."

"Some of them must have wanted just you," she said quietly.

He half smiled. "Desire on one side isn't enough. I don't want anyone but you."

Her eyes searched his in the sudden stillness. Inside, the band was playing a love song, soft and sweet and achingly haunting.

He moved closer, still not touching her, but close enough that she had to look up to see his face.

"Damn it, do I have to say the words?" he groaned out.

Her lips fell open. She hung there, trembling, her eyes like a startled fawn's, wide and unblinking.

"I love you, Amanda," he said in a voice like dark velvet, his gaze holding hers, his face taut with barely leashed emotion.

Tears burned her eyes again just before they overflowed and trailed down her cheeks, silver in the dim light.

She lifted her arms, trembling, her lips trying to form words and failing miserably.

He didn't seem to need them. He reached out and caught her up against his taut body, his arms crushing her to him as his mouth found hers blindly and took it in a wild, passionate silence that seemed to blaze up like a forest fire between them.

Her fingers tangled in the cool strands of hair at his nape, her nails lightly scraping against the tense muscles there, her mouth moaning under his, parting, inviting a penetration that caused her slender, aching body to arch recklessly toward his in blatant sensuality.

"Say it," he ground out against her mouth, his voice rasping in the darkness.

"I love you, too," she whispered breathlessly. "Hopelessly, deathlessly..." The rest became a muffled gasp as he kissed her again, his mouth rough and then gentle, tender, as it asked questions and received sweet answers all without a word being spoken.

His mouth slid against her soft, tear-stained cheek to come to rest at her ear, his arms contracting warmly at her back, his breath coming as hard and erratic as her own.

"Let's get something straight right now," he whispered gruffly. "When I said you were mine, I meant for life, and I'm going to put two rings on your finger to prove it. Oh, God, Amanda, I want so much more than the pleasure we're going to give each other in the darkness. I want to share my life with you, and have you share yours with me. I want to hold you when you hurt and dry the tears when you cry. I want to watch you laughing when we play, and see the light in your eyes when we love each other. I want to give you children and watch them grow up on Casa Verde." He drew back and looked down at her with a light in his eyes that she'd waited for, prayed for. "I love you almost beyond bearing, did you know that? I've hurt you because I was hurting. Wanting you, needing you, because you were forever running away. Don't you think it's time you stopped?" His arms drew her up closer. "Marry me. Live with me. You're the air in my lungs, Amanda. Without you, I'd stop breathing."

She smiled at him through her tears. "It's that way with me, too," she managed brokenly. "I want everything with you. I want to give you everything I have."

"All I want is your heart, love," he said softly, bending. "I'll gladly trade you mine for it."

Her lips trembled as they welcomed his, and the stars went out while she kissed him back as if she were dying, as if they were parting forever and this was the last kiss they would ever share.

She could feel his body taut with longing, feel his heartbeat like muffled thunder against her softness as his hands moved lazily, tenderly on her body and made it tremble with sweet hungers. Her fingers tangled in his black hair and clung, holding his mouth even closer over hers, feeling the smooth fabric of his evening jacket against her bare arms as he shifted her and brought her even closer.

"Are you sure my heart's all you want?" she whispered unsteadily against his devouring mouth, bursting with the joy of loving and being loved, the newness of possession.

He chuckled softly, his face changed, his eyes soft with what he was feeling. "Not quite," he admitted. "The only thing that's saving you right now is that I can't make love to you here."

Her teeth nipped lovingly at his sensuous lower lip. "You could take me home and love me."

"Oh, I intend to," he murmured with a wicked smile. "But not," he added, "until I can get Duncan and Mother out of the way for a few days. And that won't happen until after the wedding, Miss Carson, if I know my mother."

Her dark eyes laughed up at him, loving him. "Back seats are very popular," she pointed out.

"Not with me," he informed her.

"There are motels..."

He looked down his arrogant nose at her and lifted an eyebrow. "Trying to seduce me, Amanda?"

She flushed lightly. "As a matter of fact, I am."

He studied her soft, slightly swollen mouth, and his arms wrapped around her in warm affection. "You came pretty close to it last night," he reminded her, letting his darkening eyes drop to the bodice of her gown. "I'll carry that memory around in my head like the dog-eared picture of you I've carried around in my wallet for the past seven years."

Her eyes widened. "You have a picture of me?"

He nodded. "One Duncan snapped of you, running, with your hair in a glorious tangle and your skirts flying...smiling with the sun shining out of you. I'd like to have you painted like that. My God, it was so beautiful I stole it right out of his room, and felt guilty for a week."

She managed an incredulous smile. "But why didn't you just ask him for it?"

"He'd have known why I wanted it." He brushed his lips gently against her forehead. "Doe-eyes, I've loved you for so long," he whispered. "Even when I told myself I hated you, it was only because I was hurting. Every time you ran, it hurt me more. And then you made that crack about Duncan, the day I got hurt. I'd have done anything to get the truth out of you. I couldn't live with the thought that he'd touched you the way I wanted to."

"You kissed me," she recalled with a lazy smile, reliving that delicious interlude.

"It was like flying," he said gently, his eyes searching, loving. "Holding you, touching you…I'd waited years, and it was worth every one of them, until I let the doubts seep in again and scare you off. I've never trusted women very much, Amanda. It's been hell learning to trust again." His hands caressed her back gently.

"I'll never betray you," she said firmly. "You're all I'll ever want, Jason, despite my mother…"

He silenced her with a quick, rough kiss. "We'll go to the wedding—would you like that?" he asked curtly. "Amanda, if you were already married, I'd like to think I could keep my hands off you, but I don't know. I'm not sure I could. Maybe it was like that with your mother." He shrugged his broad shoulders. "I never dreamed I'd love you like this," he said, his eyes narrow. "I never realized how much I did until that night you and Duncan flew back late from New York. I prayed like I'd never prayed, and when you were back and safe all I could do was yell."

"But you came to me," she whispered, flushing with the memory.

"And we loved each other," he whispered back, bending to brush his mouth against hers tantalizingly. "The sweetest, slowest, softest loving I've ever known with a woman. The first time between us is going to be like that," he murmured, holding her eyes, watching the shy embarrassment flush her high cheekbones. "I'm going to take all night with you."

"Jason!" She hid her hot face against his chest, hearing the hard heavy beat of his heart under her ear.

"I'll make it beautiful for you," he whispered, cradling her against him.

"Every time you touch me, it *is* beautiful," she said breathlessly, her eyes closing. "I do love you so, Jason!"

"Just don't ever stop," he murmured. His arms tightened. "Don't ever stop."

"*Now* can I tell her how glad I'll be to have her for a sister-in-law?" came a humorous voice from behind them.

Jace laughed, letting Amanda turn in his possessive arms to face Duncan. "I'll even let you be the best man," Jace promised.

"On a temporary basis, of course," Duncan amended with a wry grin. "Mother's already planning the wedding. She, uh, happened to pass by the window a couple of minutes ago."

"You dragged her there, you mean." Amanda laughed.

"Not dragged, exactly," the younger man protested. "More like...led. Anyway, when are you going to make it official?"

"In about five minutes," Jace said, feeling Amanda tense. "Before she changes her mind."

"That will be never," she promised over her shoulder, melting at the look in the silver eyes that met hers.

Duncan laughed softly. "I was just remembering back a few years," he explained, noticing the puzzled looks. "When Amanda was calling you 'cowboy' and you were calling her 'Lady.' Ironic."

"She is quite a lady," Jace murmured, smiling at her, and it was no insult this time.

"And as cowboys go," Amanda returned, "he'd be my choice to ride the range with."

"Well, if you two will excuse me, I think I'll go and have a toast with that cute little Sullevan girl. Uh, you might stay away from that window, by the way." Duncan grinned as he turned away. "I think Mother's standing there."

"Duncan," Amanda called.

He turned, "Hmmmm?"

"Why did you really ask me down here with Terry? Why did you offer us the account?"

Duncan grinned from ear to ear. "Because when you left here six months ago, I just happened to notice that Jace walked around in a perpetual temper and swore every time your name was mentioned. I figured he had it so bad that a little helping hand might improve his disposition. So I gave your very helpful partner a call." He looked from one of them to the other. "And they say Cupid carries a bow. Ridiculous. He carries a telephone, of course, so that he can get people together. See you later, big brother," he added with a wink at Jace.

Jace returned it with a smile, and Amanda saw, not for the first time, the very real affection that existed between the two brothers.

"Feel like breaking the news now?" Jace asked at her ear. "I want to tell them all that you belong to me."

She turned. "I always have, you know," she whispered.

He caught her up against him and kissed her again, his mouth warm and slow and achingly thorough. At the window, inside the ballroom, a silver-haired lady was smiling happily, already working out the arrangements for the first christening in her mind.

Choose the romance that suits your reading mood

Romance

Harlequin® Romance
The anticipation, the thrill of the chase and the sheer rush of falling in love!

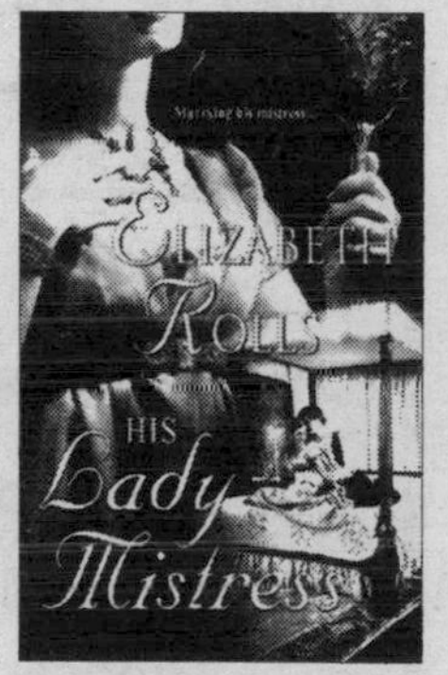

Harlequin® Historical
Roguish rakes and rugged cowboys capture your imagination in these stories where chivalry still exists!

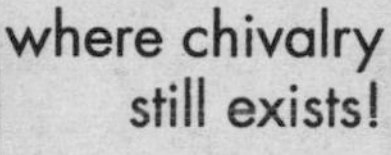

Harlequin's officially licensed NASCAR series
The rush of the professional race car circuit; the thrill of falling in love.

Look for these and many other Harlequin and Silhouette romance books wherever books are sold, including most bookstores, supermarkets, drugstores and discount stores.

SMPNASROMANCERI

THE HARLEQUIN FAMOUS FIRSTS COLLECTION™

THIS LIMITED-EDITION 12-BOOK COLLECTION FEATURES SOME OF THE FIRST HARLEQUIN® BOOKS BY *NEW YORK TIMES* BESTSELLING AUTHORS OF TODAY!

Available March:

The Matchmakers by Debbie Macomber
Tangled Lies by Anne Stuart
Moontide by Stella Cameron
Tears of the Renegade by Linda Howard

Available June:

State Secrets by Linda Lael Miller
Uneasy Alliance by Jayne Ann Krentz
Night Moves by Heather Graham
Impetuous by Lori Foster

Available September:

The Cowboy and the Lady by Diana Palmer
Fit To Be Tied by Joan Johnston
Captivated by Carla Neggers
Bronze Mystique by Barbara Delinsky

Available wherever books are sold.

www.eHarlequin.com

FFLISTBPA